JAIL BAIT

JAIL BAIT

Dorothy Cariker Cart

SUNSTONE
PRESS

Santa Fe
New Mexico

Printed in the United States of America

Library of Congress Cataloging - in - Publication Data:

Cart, Dorothy Cariker, 1923-
   Jailbait / Dorothy Cariker Cart. — 1st ed.
      p. cm.
   ISBN 0-86534-197-4 : $10.95
   1. Teenagers—Ozark Mountains Region—Fiction. 2. Satanism—Ozark
Mountains Region—Fiction. 3. Ozark Mountains Region—Fiction.
I.Title. II. Title: Jailbait.
PS3553.A7685J3   1994
813' .54—dc20   93-13562
                                                     CIP

Published by   Sunstone Press
                 Post Office Box 2321
                 Santa Fe, NM 87504-2321 / USA
                 (505) 988-4418 orders only (800) 243-5644

This progeny of my imagination is dedicated to my previous most cherished creations: Lynn, Mark and Carla and to sweet Sheri, Helen, Inez and all the others who held my hand through dark passages. . . .

CHAPTER I

Rattling and backfiring, the Kingsville school bus struggled up the Ozark Mountains above the lovely Buffalo River Country of Northwest Arkansas. Gus, the grizzled driver, frantically shifted gears as the ancient vehicle sputtered and tried to die. Head-motioning back toward his busload of boisterous Seniors, he grumbled to Miss Cobb, the Senior Sponsor and his third cousin: "Danged vacation vapors done turnt 'em into animals, Edith!"

Edith Cobb's protruding eyeballs and front teeth made her resemble a cornered rat to the lone eighth-grader in the crowd, Shannon Ceranda. Enjoying every second of the horseplay among nearby Senior boys, Shannon even laughed again when the valleys below repeated the hilarious remarks by echo with eerie vibrations.

As the bus lurched and almost stopped, Randy Smith, the lone Viet Nam veteran in the class, yelled, "Find a gear, Gus!" He snickered suggestively, "Put it in Grandma, Man!" Watching Shannon, he yodeled in his smart-alecky voice, "Old fool gonna let us run backasswards offa this mountain." Randy ignored Miss Cobb's usually inhibiting stare, thrown straight at his smart-mouth like an icicle spear. His sandy head had already swiveled back to the rear where the girls sat, and her withering scorn singed not a hair of his puny ponytail nor the rubber band holding it. The Senior with the attention span of a first-grader continued talking, gesticulating, and performing the Funky Chicken to Connie Coger's loud radio rock 'n roll music.

"Times like this I'm glad my hearin' left me," Gus yelled. "Now, I can't hear this ole bucket of bolts backfar--or even to myself sometimes!" He cackled like a sissified rooster.

Miss Cobb's studied dignity ignored his uncouth humor. Shaking her bluish Brillo-pad perm, the teacher confided to Gus, "Maybe exploring Skull Cave with the Senior Class wasn't the best idea the Principal ever had, especially with older guys like Randy. Control could be a problem." To sixteen-year-old

Shannon Ceranda, watching the action with an eighth-grader's fascination, Miss Cobb's view seemed archaic, limited by spinsterhood.

Glancing quickly toward Randy while fighting the wheel to miss a pothole, Gus grouched, "Even 'fore Nam, thatun didn't have the sense God give a goose!"

"Well, the Principal decreed the cave trip or nothing for the Seniors this year," the teacher said, looking glum, "but I notice he didn't come along."

Gus stroked his gray handlebars thoughtfully then shifted his cud of tobacco and the gear simultaneously, "Yow, I know," he grumbled. "An, from the way this crate drives, he shoulda spent that chicken feed on this bus." He wiped sweat with a greasy hand, then his khakis, adding to existing black parentheses by each pocket.

Shannon's excitement accelerated as she gazed in awe over the panorama of mountain peaks clad in newborn April finery. Far below their lofty path, the Buffalo River girdled the narrow valley with a rhinestone belt of sunlit ripples. Soaring white cliffs walled meadows by the river on one side while mountains snuggled up to farm homes along the road into Boxley on the other side. Magic Mountain, aptly named, decided the eighth grader. *Not only the zenith of my life; the boundary between my sheltered Kings River Valley childhood and my adventure as a young woman on her own for the first time! I can't believe I'm really here with these neat Senior hunks who look at me hungrily.*

Through the open window, her tilted nose garnered messages of woodsy glens, blossoming wild grape and clear mountain streams. She felt herself tingle with awakening sensuality as the muscular hard-bodies of the Senior boys eddied around her. Glorying in the feel of freshly shampooed hair, she allowed the April breeze to swirl its gardenia scented tendrils across her eyes, letting them feast on the myriad coppery lights in the sun. She scooted forward in the seat, enjoying the feeling as her hair rippled down below her waist. *What incredible magic allowed me to get the lead in the Senior play--to be envied to the max by my eighth-grade-friends-then, above all--to be invited on this Senior Trip? She* wondered again if her teacher had chosen her to compensate for time lost to Mono and its complications.

She smiled to herself at thought of her family's concern about her readiness to share this cave exploration with Seniors. Keith, her older brother with his affectionate kidding: "You know `boy craziness' hits a lotta girls your age. In April, the sap rises, you know. Don't let it rise in you, kiddo!" *Like my brothers and their friends hadn't cured me of any fool notions about guys.*

Big, blond and blowzy Connie Coger turned her radio down enough to yell above nearby banter to Shannon: "Girl, I hope you realize these Senior boys ain't got but one thang on their so-called minds. An they're gonna think little Shannon's a push-over, being just a eighth-grader." Shannon shook her head, wondering if the chubby twenty-year-old had actually ever had a date, let alone besieged by even one horny male among these great looking Seniors. Too bad Connie doesn't watch her weight, thought Shannon; she has a lovely face.

Shannon lowered long lashes to hide the laughter that usually surfaced in her green eyes. "You think for a minute, Connie, that Keith and Tim would allow little sis to make the Senior Trip without plenty of advice? Not to mention my dad, the setting hen of all time where his one gal-chick is concerned."

"The girls wanta talk to you, Connie," called Randy Smith, who had been pacing in the aisle near the girls in his hyperactive way for a few minutes.

"See what I mean, girl?" Connie whispered to Shannon. "No wonder his daddy named him Randy. I'll move in a minute, but you watch yourself. That little rooster drags his wing at every chick in sight!"

As the old yellow bus passed a pasture where a roan bull rode a heifer, Randy shouted at the cattle, "You lazy stud! Quit making' that gal carry you up the mountain!" Some of the other boys laughed, but Miss Cobb turned an icy stare Randy's way. His burro-bray of laughter still continued.

Dislodging her flowered dress from its hip-grip, Connie moved across the aisle where another Senior girl sat, and Randy raced for the vacant seat, beating out two other Senior boys who had the same idea. Looking triumphant, he whipped out a pack of cigarettes from the pocket of his chambray work shirt, deliberately nudging Shannon's right breast with his elbow.

Looking at her with a phoney heavy-lidded look, he made a production out of lighting up. As Monty Villines and Kevin Wahl kidded and cuffed each other in the aisle, Randy motioned their way and drawled in his deepest bass: "Act like bull mooses in heat don't they, Red? You know--showin' off for the females?" He nudged her again, holding his skinny elbow against her.

The sixteen-year-old moved away from him as far as the cold metal permitted. Fanning away his cigarette smoke, she coughed, then answered coldly, "I hate that nickname, almost as much as I detest cigarette smoke."

"Well, la-te-da!" he smirked. He blew rings of smoke across the aisle toward Connie, who gave him a coy smile and fluffed her blond hair. When he lifted his left arm to wipe his oily, acne-scarred cheek, Shannon got an overpowering dose of stale sweat. "I know Shannon's jail bait," he wisecracked to Monty and the other Seniors watching from the aisle. He turned back to Shannon.

"Redheads always turn me on," he confided in her ear. "An I'll overlook uppity talk from a leggy redhead any time, especially with a body like yourn."

"Excuse me," she said, trying to rise. "I'm moving back with the others."

Grabbing her jeans at the back waistband, he pulled her down to the seat, letting his hand linger, forcing her to sit on it.

"You'd better let me go!" she threatened in a low voice, hoping to avoid a scene. He merely blew more smoke her way, daring her to cause trouble.

"Too dammed bad yore mind ain't as growed up as yore bod, kid!" he taunted.

"Move your hand!" she ordered through clenched teeth.

His tone had turned spiteful. "Temper! Temper! I've always heard about passionate redheads. Too bad you think you're better'n me. Well, you wouldn't have that there creamy skin with red hair if you had to do farm work like most girls around here. Even them big green eyes wouldn' t look so good if you was speckled as a guinea egg."

"Let me out!" she demanded, struggling up and tramping hard on his boots. "I may live in a big house, but I work. We have a big farm, so what? Just means more work, and I've helped ever since I got well. I work alongside my brothers." He eyed her contemptuously from under heavy, lashless lids:

"Yow, I bet! Me 'n my hill brothers fought in 'Nam so guys like them brothers of yourn could stay on that big farm and live the good life. Now you look down on me an them." His mouth narrowed, resembling a cracked pumpkin.

Before she could protest the lie, Monty Villines stood looking down at him. "Back off, Randy!" he warned, dark eyes flashing. "You're way outa line here." His broad-shouldered build made Randy's gangly height look puny. The older man gave Monty a long insolent look, but Randy's pale eyes quailed before the other's angry stare. Cigarette dangling from pouty lips, Randy rose and affected a jaunty stroll through the silent crowd, holding his greasy ponytail at a defiant angle.

Shannon's heart lilted as Monty dropped into the seat beside her. Surely he has no idea of the parts he has played in my fantasies since the Senior Play, she thought, pulse racing at the touch of their shoulders. Just looking at him gave her a rush, a rocket ride she had never experienced even in her first bumbling boy-kiss at fourteen. For a second, she felt her first inkling of the force her father and brothers had cautioned against, calling it "Boy Craziness".

"Just try to ignore ole Randy," Monty whispered. "Got messed up on drugs in 'Nam. Mostly going to school because the government pays him to."

"Yes, my brother told me drugs probably gave his cheeks those strange vertical creases." He nodded, studying her closely before continuing.

"Anyway, hope he didn't ruin your trip. I'm glad you came. And I thought you were great in the play." She wanted to dive into the mysterious darkness of his eyes and never come up for air, in spite of her breathlessness. To her consternation, she felt a rising blush. *Oh no, he's going to think I'm just a kid.*

'"Aw, thanks," she protested. "But not really. I love acting but have no training. You could probably tell that I was scared spitless too!" *I'm talking too much, but I can't seem to stop under the spell of those eyes.* "I'm surprised I remembered my lines. Stage fright usually constipates my—um—mind." The word "constipates" stopped her monologue. *Why'd I have to use that word; no wonder Mama says I talk like a field hand from being only with boys all summer.*

"That's better than getting Diarrhea of the Mouth, I reckon," he drawled, then laughed heartily. Oh dear, she thought, do you suppose he meant me and my chattering? But the sound of his laughter and the admiration in those marvelous dark eyes made her heart do flips. *So this is what my brothers meant by 'Boy Crazy'? Wow! No wonder Dad worried. No wonder people are so obsessed with sex on television.* This is like doing a slalom from the top of Magic Mountain, she thought as their eyes locked. Then, from the corner of her eye, Shannon caught sight of Miss Cobb standing and yelling in their direction with the large goiter bobbing on her freckled neck, but her anger was directed at Randy. To Shannon's relief, composure returned when she interpreted Miss Cobb's shrill command: "Get rid of that cigarette, Randy Smith!"

Monty seemed oblivious to surveillance or any other distraction as he murmured close to her ear, "I liked the way you looked on stage in that green dress. Those gorgeous green eyes moved me even more than your acting."

Seeing the chaperone's eyes swivel their way, Shannon snapped her fingers in mock exasperation, hating to break the spell but fearing Miss Cobb's humiliation. "And to think I wore jeans today," she said. "Mama begged me to wear a dress. But Dad says, `Let her wear jeans, Josie. I want her to look exactly like another Senior boy.'"

"Come on," he countered. "Senior boys are stupid sometimes, but not that stupid." Shannon felt capable of dedicating her career to inspiring that wonderful deep laughter that crinkled those darkly fringed eyes. She decided to ignore Miss Cobb and dare to live dangerously.

"Tell me about Skull Cave," she urged. "Have you ever been in it?" *How does his presence excite me so?*

"Oh sure, since I live nearby. But, actually, only once. There's always been a lot of mystery about it. Rumors of weird goings-on, you know. Especially since the war and all the drug activity hereabouts."

"Dad told me it used to be called Devil's Den before they found the skull in the cave and changed the name."

"Yes, you know how superstitious us mountaineers can be?" Monty cocked an eyebrow at her, grinning.

"My dad must've heard a lot of tales. He's really spooked about it." *He sparks my creative combustion.*

"As you probably know, an earthquake shut off parts of it after Confederate soldiers used it during the Civil War. So a lot of it has never been explored."

"Is it safe now?" she asked, not really alarmed but angling for his protectiveness. She saw the look she craved in his eyes.

"I think so; the County Engineers cleared the passages we're gonna explore about two months ago. They braced it up some, but only near the entrances. The cave is rumored to run for miles, and nobody knows what may be in there. It's on private property, a farm belonging to Mrs. Edmonson."

"Yes, I met her while we were practicing for the play. I'll have her for English next year."

We're camping in her old farmhouse right near the Skull Cave entrance."

"I think it's so exciting. What an adventure!"

"Well, I have to warn you. A lot of people around here wouldn't go in that mountain on a bet! And that includes my dad. He's one of the Black Villines clan who's afraid of no man or beast. Ole Dal would ride the meanest bull or bronc, but Dallas Villines is afraid of things he can't see. He'd never admit it, but you'd have to hogtie him to get him in Skull Cave."

"I never knew his name was Dallas."

"Yow, my family sorta has a thing for western names. Dad named me 'Montana', and I have an Uncle Utah, sorta famous in rodeo circles."

"I just now realize why they say 'Black Villines' when talking about your family," she admitted, longing to touch the bluish-black ducktails that tried to curl behind his ears. "Most of the Villines over Kingsville way are blondish. As a kid, I conjured up this scarey image of your side of the family; I thought they were saying 'Black Villains'."

She laughed, her eyes on his beautifully curved lips, the way they tilted slightly at the corners just before he smiled.

"Some of us are," he teased, "But, as I was saying, I helped cart out some artifacts several years ago from the main part of the cave. I found one of those huge iron kettles used to store powder for the Confederates. Some of the farmers,mostly my relatives along the Buffalo, still use 'em to feed livestock. There's ore cars and tracks in there used to haul out bat manure."

"Whatever for?" she asked.

"For ammo before the Civil War ended. That stuff has nitrogen in it, I think. Anyway, they used it to make ammunition." Watching his large hands as he talked, using them expressively, Shannon wondered how he could play a guitar and violin so masterfully. *Slender, long fingers, beautifully shaped.* She could almost feel them caressing her body. Daydreaming, she realized, she hadn't heard what he was saying.

She jerked herself back to the lovely reality as he went on: "The Villines were French Huguenots. Protestants driven to America around 1700 by religious persecution. Came on to Arkansas about the same time as your great grandparents, I believe."

"Did you get your musical talent from the Villines side?"

"Yes, such as it is. Many were musicians. In fact, one was court musician at Versailles palace near Paris. Lost his head in the French Revolution, along with King Louis XV, I think it was. I'm not really sure which Louie it was."

"You sure he didn't lose his head over Louis, the Sun King?" she teased. "He had gorgeous long curls and lacy undies. At least I read that somewhere." *Looking at him sets my fantasies free.*

"Maybe, he was a gay caballero," he admitted, "but if he was like me, he preferred Marie Antoinette. And she probably told him to go eat cake!"

She laughed. "Seems your humor is about as rare as your musical talent. I'd never really seen you perform until the night of the Senior Play," she said. "I was impressed. Oh, I'd heard my brothers compare your playing to Chet Atkins. Tim even says your voice is better than Neil Diamond's, his hero!"

"Wow! I wish!" he said, looking pleased. Modestly, he changed the subject. "I discovered our grandpas came to the Buffalo River country together when I helped put the Senior History project together."

"I know; isn't it exciting?" *Destiny working to intertwine our fate,* Shannon thought smugly.

"Did you know your Grandpa Steel was mentioned in my grandpa's journals? He calls him 'Judge Steel'. And the creek into our ranch is named for him. How about that?" He hesitated,"Well,I guess he was actually your great grandpa?"

"I knew Mama's grandpa was a circuit judge, riding around on horses and dispensing justice, but I didn't know about the creek. I'd like to see it!"

"Believe me, you will!" he promised, giving her an intent look.

"Just think—we're practically related'" Shannon said, reveling in his eye messages.

"Thank God, we're not," he added reverently. They were still gazing into each other's eyes, lost to the hubbub on the old bus when Connie nudged Shannon, breaking 'the spell.

"Come back here quick with me," the big blonde urged. "Miss Cobb is watchin' you like a hawk stalkin' a chicken."

"She's got me sized up right," Shannon admitted dryly, rising reluctantly to follow, hoping Monty hadn't heard her being summoned like a naughty child.

CHAPTER II

Connie slumped down in the bus' back seat, resembling a sofa in her flowered chintz dress. She motioned Shannon into the seat beside her with an irritating, patronizing air. I probably know as much about men as she does, thought Shannon, after observing the girl's response to Randy's crude advances. Her suspicions as to Connie's maturity seemed confirmed when she observed that the blonde had drawn a heart on a note pad. Her affected writing, full of fancy curlicues and circles for dots, read "Randy & Connie". Then, the girl had written "Mrs. Randy Smith", and "Connie Faye Smith".

Shannon studied Connie's cherubic face curiously, motioning toward the note pad. "Do you actually like Randy?"

Connie put the note pad in her big purse hurriedly. "No," she shrugged. Shannon's directness seemed to disconcert the other girl. "Um, he's O.K." She squirmed uneasily. "He's well—kinda cool-like—you know—been around. I've always preferred older men." Under Shannonn's searching survey, she bridled:

"Well,like—I know he's not in your class, but he treats me better'n most guys."

"You gotta be kiddin!" Shannon blurted. "What do you mean 'my class'—not in the eighth grade?"

"Aw, stop with the hogwash. I live in a lowsy mobile home on a bare hill, and you—you live in a huge house with white columns looking down on the whole valley."

"I don't 'look down' on anyone and neither does my family. We're all just farmers." Shannon could see the older girl becoming more defensive.

"Don't look at me like I just fell off a turnip wagon somers," Connie blurted. "I can see you think you're better'n me. I can see you think Monty Villines likes you too. But you're just foolin' yourself. That Missy Evans set her cap for him long ago and, believe me, she's got him by the shirttail on a downhill pull." Her pasty broad face had become splotched with anger, and she glared pointedly at Missy, who had joined Monty and was hanging on his right shoulder from the bus seat vacated by Shannon. Connie's voice took on the honeyed Southern accent affected by Melissa, "An you-all know whatevah Missy wants, Missy gets. Aftah awl, I got the charm, mannahs, land, an all that money, honey." The girl's sudden anger seemed totally out of character with her usual bland affability. Shannon had often wondered how Connie could survive her reported abuse at home, yet appear so pleasant. She must be totally out of touch with her real feelings, thought Shannon, resolving to be more tolerant.

Now, feeling a stab of her first identifiable jealousy, Shannon asked, "Does he actually date her, or does she do all the pursuing?" As she watched the bodaciously beautiful blonde flutter long lashes up at Monty, she turned blind with rage.

"Oh, she pursues him plenty! Who wouldn't if encouraged? He's quite a hunk, isn't he? As you can see, she's all over him ever chanct. Lookit the bitch!" Connie's voice became even more nasal and Ozarky. "Lookit her battin' them big brown Cocker eyes. Cher-rist, reminds me of a blonde Cocker bitch daddy had. Peed like a puppy ever time he looked at her!"

To avoid another painful stab of jealousy, Shannon resolved never to look toward Monty and Missy again as Miss Cobb made her way down the aisle, but she found herself hoping the teacher intended to humiliate Missy. Instead, Miss Cobb dropped down in the seat beside Shannon.

Pinning Shannon down with those prominent eyes, she began in what seemed an unusually loud volume: "I've been watching you, Shannon."

Gulping, Shannon struggled to meet the teacher's eyes, feeling like a dove pointed by a birddog.

"Oh, really. Why? What did I do?"

"Oh, nothing, dear," the spinster hurriedly reassured the redhead. "I just realize you're awfully young to be dealing with older young men. These Senior boys *are* adolescents and they're—well—aggresive sexually—and I promised your father I'd watch after you." Shannon stole a glance toward Monty to see if he was listening. To her chagrin, Missy seemed to be straining to hear, even shushing the loud laughter nearby. Struck temporarily dumb, Shannon leaned very close to the teacher, hoping she would compensate by lowering her voice, but Miss Cobb seemed to believe the eighth-grader suffered hearing loss.

"Um, as I was saying," she droned on in a very loud tone, "your dad told me that he'd discussed situation ethics with you before you left. regarding keeping boys—er—in line, but I'm not sure you've ever been confronted with anything like this situation. Most of these boys wouldn't take advantage of you but—" She cleared her throat and twitched nervously.

"Oh, my word, Miss Cobb! My dad! I should've known. He's such an old maid!" The teacher looked suddenly stricken, rubbing her splotchy goiter in a flustered way. Then, it dawned on Shannon that the term "old maid" might be offensive to this spinster. That's all I need, she thought, feeling herself flushing.

"Um, what I meant is—um—I know adolescent sex is a real dead-end road. Some of my friends have already ended up that way tied to some local yokel before they even know who they are—much less what they want outa life. Having babies and becoming slaves with no way out. Not me, No way, José! *Oh no!* " She smote her brow. *Now, she probably thinks I'm disrespectful.* Then she added weakly, "That's what I tell Mom. Mom's name is Josie."

The wattle under the teacher's chin turned red and quivered with agitation. "Oh well, oh sure, yes," interjected Miss Cobb nervously, rising like a hen turkey ready to take flight. "I just had no idea you were so mature."

"Believe me," Shannon added in a tone fueled by anger, "I don't need to have sex with a Senior or anyone else to make me feel good about myself!" Sudden silence on the bus made Shannon blush.

"Way to go, girl!" Connie squealed in her ear as Miss Cobb scuttled away. "Bet Cobb never had a date; she oughta ast you how to handle' em. Specially ole Randy Smith!".

CHAPTER III

Gus pulled the old bus across the singing shallows of a small stream, parking it close to an unpainted, sprawling farmhouse nestled at the foot of Magic Mountain. Mrs. Edmonson, the other sponsor, stood on the porch wearing a sunbonnet to protect a sensitive skin, subject to sun tumors.

"Hi Everyone!" she yodeled. "This is it! Everybody grab your camping gear!" Holding an apronful of apples, she ran to greet the group with her ample body parts seeming to applaud their arrival. As the seniors dived for apples in her apron, she panted to Miss Cobb: "I've been busier than a one-armed paperhanger this afternoon. Hadn't cleaned this ole house since I moved out to teach at Kingsville. Talk about a chore! Then I got Delbert to help me move in cots and groceries." She stopped to pant, "then we cleaned out the well."

Shannon gazed around, awed at the beauty of this cove in springtime. Dogwood and redbud bloomed among the shiny new leaves of the surrounding woodland. An old apple tree, gnarled and twisted from weathering many winters, still filled the air with its blossoming sweetness. Nearby, a maple extended an invitation for climbing with a limb across one corner of the sagging, wrap-around porch. Its newborn leaves still showed magenta wombs at their centers from which the greenery had unfurled. Mayapple, wild violet, ivy, and fern led up to the gaping maw of Skull Cave on the west side of the clear brook. A pair of bluebirds celebrated a nestful of gaping bills with warbles.

As Shannon tossed her backpack on the porch and stood looking at Skull Cave, she shivered involuntarily. The cave's cavernous mouth seemed to be drooling green bile between its stalagmite and stalactite teeth. Yuk, she thought, imagining it's mossy tunnels.

"What's wrong, girl?" Connie asked, following Shannon's fascinated gaze. "Surely you're not cold!" She sniffed her own armpits. "I'm sweatin' like a sow."

"No, it's just that—well it's even spookier looking than I expected. I've never been in a cave before. What if it gives me claustrophobia?"

"Aw, you only git that if you git bat bit."

"That's hydrophobia, silly! Actually, I was mostly thinking of all the things Dad told me to try to scare me out of doing this. I thought he was more scared I couldn't handle older boys than spelunking. Now, I'm wondering if I shouldn't have listened to those tales of things that went on in that mountain in the past."

"Like what?" Connie asked with rounded eyes. Before Shannon could answer, Monty asked Shannon to help him gather firewood. Spacing out at thought of being alone with him in the forest, she felt mixed emotions when Connie invited herself to acompany them.

Only conscious effort kept Shannon from watching every move Monty made. *The way those Wranglers fit his athletic body. Maybe Dad had a point about my being able to handle at least one older fellow. Maybe Keith wasn't just being a smartalec older brother in warning me about not letting the sap rise. Oh my Lord, I think I can feel it when I glance at that bronzed face under that white Stetson! Could a first crush be this powerful?*

As they strolled through the dappled shade, Connie plied Monty with many questions about Randy Smith as to who he dated or liked. Obviously non-commital, he seemed to discourage Connie's interest, probably knowing the girl might be badly hurt. Loading his arms with wood, he urged: "Let's get this wood back so the cooks can get busy. I'm starving, and so are the others." Connie rose laboriously from the log where she had settled, following reluctantly.

As darkness fell, Shannon and Monty sat on the limb of the old apple tree, swinging their legs, seduced by the fragrance of blossoms and the music of the stream. Watching the stars appear, Shannon yearned to capture the moment to hold forever. *Maybe I'll tell our children about this someday.* Dream on, fool, she warned herself.

"Listen to the whippoorwills up that hollow," he said, tilting his head.

She listened dreamily. "I love twilight. It's like the universe tunes up that time of day to play earthlings a lullabye." His dark eyes met hers with complete understanding. "I would have been afraid anyone else would laugh at my fantasies," she admitted.

"I know," he said. "I even wrote a song about it once. My favorite time of day always. My lyrics went something like this." He hummed a few bars and looked around to be sure the others had gone inside the farmhouse. He cleared his throat self-consciously. "I called it 'Twilight Time." And she knew this was something as intimate to him as her revelations about twilight had been. *He too feels this contagious combution.*

"Twilight time falls softly like the dew upon my stress-taut, anxious mind, Gentling, healing, peaceful—to renew body, mind and spirit of mankind. Fretting babies quiet in its spell and snuggle close to mothers' breasts; In farmhouse, highrise or robins' nests, Mothers beam upon their young at rest. Myriad tiny creature voices blend in meadow-mountain lullabye, hushed by the Maestro on high, who soothes His own children when they cry."

"How absolutely lovely," she breathed softly. "So beautiful it makes me cry!" Then he kissed her, and it seemed the cicadia, whippoorwill-frog chorus had turned into the Hallelujah Chorus. He kissed her lips, her brimming tears, her throat, and she never wanted him to stop. *A feeling of profound melding.*

Reality shattered the spell as Mrs. Edmonson's nasal voice yelled: "Git in here 'fore I throw these taters and onions out to the dogs!"

"Wow, they smell great;" Monty said. "But I'm a lot hungrier for more of what we just shared." Reluctantly, they climbed down to the porch, went inside.

With the breeze from the brook, the crackling fire in the wide field-stone fireplace felt good as the group roasted weiners to go with the fried potatoes and onions on their paper plates. Most of them sat on their bedrolls and sleeping bags on the plank floor. Mrs. Edmonson pointed out craters in the stone hearth where children of her family had cracked hickory nuts and black walnuts from their woodland for generations.

"I hope you-all are as excited as I am about tomorrow's explorations" she exclaimed, "I've always wondered what might be under our mountain. But my parents always warned us kids not to venture in there, And then so much of it was closed off for almost a century."

"What do you think a person might find?" Gus asked, aiming an expert squirt of ambeer at the ashes. He cut off another chew from his plug of tobacco. "I've heared of quare goin-ons since I was a youngun. My pa found that danged skull right in the cave. He an Henry Steele was coon huntin'."

"We could find anything," the teacher admitted, "even skeletons of Civil War casualties or others sealed off when a terrible earthquake shook this area. They think it happened at the time it created those bottomless cracks in the bluffs over by Harrison. You know, where Devil's Den State Park is now?"

"My dad said at one time they thought this was part of Devil's Den," Shannon remarked. Monty nodded, confirming that he had heard the same thing.

"Aw, git real! That's miles from here." Randy sneered, obviously still holding a grudge.

Missy griped: "Well, I for one don't want to go in that creepy, wet cave. I don't see why we couldn't have taken a trip like civilized people to N'Orleans. Y'all really want to risk gittin' bat-bit in some drippy, evil-smellin' hole in the ground?" She whipped out a comb and preened her blonde ponytail, eyeing Monty, posing to seductively display her breasts through her clinging blouse.

"Why don't you an me just stay here?" asked Randy, falling down beside her and sprawling over her lap like a dog showing submissiveness to another.

"I doubt your daddy could afford to send you to New Orleans, Missy," Connie snorted indignantly, "Mine barely came up with the dough for hotdogs." She sniffed to Shannon. "That Missy's so fakey they shoulda named her Polly Esther." Shannon giggled.

"Well," Missy sneered, "my father don't spend his money for houses and lots like yours, Whore houses and lots of moonshine!"Only Missy laughed at her cruel joke.

Connie shot up like a jack-in-the-box, her face turning grim and florid in the firelight as she glared at Missy. Missy grabbed her make-up mirror and bag, then flounced off toward a bedroom. But she halted as Shannon exclaimed:

"I can't wait to explore the cave. Who gets a chance for an adventure like this anymore?" Monty touched her hand on the quilt, making her pulse race.

Monty's gesture apparently was not lost on Missy, who retorted sarcastically:

"That's a dumb kid for you! A dumb boy-crazy eighthgrader."

As Missy slammed the door, Connie thumbed her nose when the chaperones weren't watching. Then she stalked out following Missy. Monty retrieved his guitar from his gear in the strained silence that followed the departure of the two girls and began strumming. Then his pleasing baritone invited everyone to join in "On Top of Old Smokey."

At the top of his lungs, Randy yodeled out his own version, obviously angling for attention: "On top of ole Smokey, all covered with soot, lay Fi-Fi, the she-bear, and she was a slut!" No one laughed, and Monty switched to the song "El Paso".

Listening to the ballad, Shannon's imagination filmed a romantic segment in the flames of the lovely valley where Monty's father raised horses. She saw herself as the lovely Felina, the Mexican maiden, and Monty the dashing young cowboy who rode through a hail of gunfire to die at her feet.

A loud commotion from the bedroom stilled Monty's guitar and the singing. Connie Coger's voice bellowed: "How dare you tell around town that I sleep with my brothers?" The reply was indistinct, but Shannon recognized Missy's syrupy drawl, "My brothers are drunken liars if they said that!" Connie roared,

"Well, everybody in Kingsville swears it's true!" Missy charged shrilly.

"You cheap bitch! You started that lie like that one about Shannon just because she beat you out for the lead in the Senior Play."

"You know she just got it 'cause her daddy's on the school board."

Disbelieving her own ears, Shannon turned to Monty, but he just shook his head and began strumming loudly to drown out the rest of the cat-fight. When he finished, he put the guitar away and looked toward the bedroom where silence reigned. "Does someone need to take the cat a saucer of milk?" he asked, grinning. The others applauded, including the sponsors.

Connie returned to the group just before Miss Cobb called "Lights Out". Looking glum, she asked Shannon to share one of the bedrooms with her. Taking one of the kerosene lamps with them, they left the living room as the others chose cots or made out sleeping bags. Shannon wondered if she could ever settle down enough to sleep after the excitement of the evening. Maybe at least I stand a better chance in here alone with Connie, she decided as she climbed into her sleeping bag. *No way I could lie down in that room with Monty and ever sleep.* In fact, she still seemed to levitate with tension above the sleeping bag for hours as she relived all that had transpired. She felt surprise that Connie could sleep after her encounter.

Her reverie ended when she heard the legs of Connie's old cot beating a nervous rhythm on the plank flooring. Her mouth dropped open in the darkness at the thought of what Connie must be doing. Then Connie sobbed, great heaving sobs, that made the cot dance to a different rhythm. Rising, Shannon knelt beside her, patting the lumpy body, searching for comforting words. "They were all angry with Missy," she whispered, "We were all rooting for you." She sat there until the other girl began to snore in an adenoidal whine.

Then she knelt by a window for hours—seeing Monty's face and expressions, trying to read her destiny in the starblaze. Alternately, she gloried in their bonding and the future together or berated herself as an adolescent victim of rising sap.

CHAPTER IV

Shannon felt relief the next morning when Mrs. Edmonson substituted Connie for Missy in Shannon's group to explore the west branch of the four main tunnels of Skull Cave. Her relief became elation when Monty became its leader because of his previous experience inside the cave as well as the scarcity of chaperones. Chagrin was added to Shannon's emotions when

Miss Cobb added Randy to their group. I must have impressed Miss Cobb with my maturity, she thought, for her to trust me with that creep. *On the other hand, and more likely, she didn't want to have to tolerate him herself or is getting even with me for talking about old maids.*

As they checked lists to be sure all supplies had been placed in backpacks, Randy walked over to Connie and commented, "Me an you gonna have to get lost in a side tunnel, Lotta-Mama!" Connie laughed and swatted him playfully. Watching, Shannon longed to slug him for taking advantage of the girl's vulnerability, hating even the echo of his Kookaburra laugh.

By this time, the rest of the seniors had gathered inside the mouth of the cave. Miss Cobb separated three other groups of students to be led by herself, Mrs. Edmonson, and Gus. Then, she pinned Monty down with her protruding eyes like a lab specimen, announcing nasally: "As you all know, Monty grew up in this area and has been chosen to lead Group Four through the west tunnel." Pointing it out on the map, she then double checked each group for working lanterns, flashlights, food, and luminous markers to guide them back to the cave entrance. Then she checked the group for sweaters, clucking like a mother hen over one scantily-clad chick.

"Honestly, Missy," she scolded. "I'd think you would've known better than to wear short shorts and a tank top in a cold place like this."

"She's just being helpful," Randy called out, "keeping us guys warm." She flounced away when he tried to hug her.

"She probably hopes to sue the State of Arkansas if she gets pneumonia," commented Connie. Missy hugged her breasts until they crested, glaring. "I'm not going in this creepy place, period!" declared the slender blonde, already blue with chill bumps. "I'm going back to bed!" As she stormed out of the cave, Connie led a cheer.

Monty gathered his group in front of the west tunnel, which looked so dark and wet that it filled Shannon with dread. If Monty had not been in the group, she would have been tempted to join Missy in retreating to the farmhouse. Unclipping a long flashlight from his belt, Monty made a production of checking their backpacks as ordered by Miss Cobb. Aiming the bright light into Shannon's purple pack, he cleared his throat with mock unctuous authority. He fished out Shannon's small makeup kit and held it aloft. "This is contraband, not on Miss Cobb's list, excess baggage. We will just leave it here until we return." He quirked one eyebrow and pressed his upper lip with his thumb. Daring her with his eyes, he placed it nearby on a shelf of rock.

Grabbing the kit from the rock, she held it behind her back. "Any cavewoman knows you don't stand a chance with cavemen without makeup!" she declared' "What we have here, gang, is a case of the blind leading the blind. He told me himself he had never been any further in this cave than where we are."

"What I said was I know as much as anyone here about this part of it," he replied, turning serious as if he realized his responsibility for the first time. "This is the tunnel that was blocked off until recently and has never been explored since the engineers cleared the debris and mud at the entrance. As Mrs. Edmonson said, we could find skeletons, Civil War artifacts, snakes."

"Snakes!" echoed Shannon. "She didn't say 'snakes'" Shivering and scanning ceiling and walls, she yodeled, "Th—That's all, folks!" imitating Woody Woodpecker. She did a comical Jackie Gleason exit maneuver. "See you back at the farmhouse tonight."

Monty grabbed her sweater and pulled her back, amending his guide's spiel. "Um, I got a little carried away with self-importance, being named a guide and all," he admitted, laughing. "Actually, there's probably nothing in here other than millions of bats to crap in your hair—and spiders."

Shannon faked a gasp, turning to leave again, but he grabbed her back-pack, Reaching inside he brought out two half-pint canning jars.

"What on earth?" he asked, looking astonished, "You canning today? Where's your pressure cooker?"

Shannon squirmed, feeling juvenile. "Naw, my little brother, Tod, has a science project that requires a bat and a spider, so I promised to get them."

Monty swatted his brow. "Wimmin!" he groaned comically. "Always cause nothing but trouble for the great white hunters on safari. Canning bats!"

At least, he called me a woman, Shannon thought as she shouldered her pack and followed the group into the slimy, narrow tunnel. Fighting claustrophobia and fear, she tried to dismiss thoughts of the millions of bats squeaking and scuffling for space on the ceiling two feet above her. Surely her father's stories of people who went mad--from being bitten by rabid bats were told only for the purpose of discouraging this trip. As her back began to hurt from stooping through some of the passage with very low ceilings, she half wished she'd listened to her father.

At times, they skirted chasms, warned by the sound of falling water from the small stream that meandered through much of this arm of the limestone passage. Monty progressed slowly, lighting each descent, warning them of stepping off into bottomless pits if they hurried too much.

"You know, there's fish in here that have no eyes," he said, pointing one out in a deeper pool. " Lost their eyes from lack of use. Let this be a warning to you about your brains as we go on to college." Their laughter seemed to release some of the tension that had kept them silent although it produced eerie echoes.

Shannon felt a twinge of pain at the thought of Monty's going away to college, *You're building yourself up for a bigger fall than if you stepped off into a bottomless pit. What chance do you have with an older guy who looks like Monty?* Grow up, she told herself, stumbling along, seeing double images of the lantern he carried. Suddenly, she stumbled over a fallen stalagmite and scraped her knees. Randy helped her up, feeling her up as he did so in the darkness.

"Stop it!" she hissed, and the tunnel magnified her whisper and repeated it. As she rubbed the lacerated denim over her bleeding knees, Monty backtracked and held his lantern over her. "What's going on?" he asked, eyeing Randy suspiciously. Randy's shrug did not match his guilty face.

"Oh, I just stumbled. Just call me `Grace'." said Shannon. Monty studied her face, looking grim as he turned on Randy.

"You know what I told you," he warned, "Jail Bait! You read me loud and clear? Roger?"

"Roger, Man," Randy repeated, adding, "Hellfire, I wasn't doin' nuthin!" His eyes stayed fixed on the tip of his long nose.

I can't believe Monty called me "Jail Bait", she thought indignantly, *Does that mean he respects me only because he's afraid not to? Well he didn't kiss me like I was a kid--or Jail Bait.*

His eyes were gentle as he looked down at her and offered, "I have first-aid stuff. Do you need something on those knees?" The concern in his deep voice awakened primitive, scary emotions. As she shook her head, he reached to the ceiling above his dark head and held forth four squirming bats that resembled newborn mice with wings, "Wanta can these?" he asked, "You see, you can't get just one in a pinch,"

"Yuk," she grimaced as he placed the babies in the jar. "Tod will be thrilled, Thanks," She returned to her recriminations about being jail bait,

As they crept along for what seemed like hours under ceiling so low that they had to crawl at times, Shannon wished her stature matched her low spirits. I'd go back if I wasn't afraid to go alone, she thought irritably. Her back pained and she felt ready to scream from claustrophobia at times, especially when her hand touched a white salamander as she crawled through a space barely large enough for the men to squeeze through.

Then they entered an area with more space and ventilation. Monty stopped and sniffed the air. "Hey, I smell smoke," he said, "or burning grass?" He brushed cobwebs from her hair, letting his hand follow its coppery fall to her waist.

"Maybe we're about to come to where it exits," Shannon said hopefully,warmed by his touch.

"Yow, or somebody's smokin' pot down the tunnel," Randy offered cheerily. He took long drags, eyes glistening.

"Well, I hope we're about to exit this place," Connie declared. "I thought my butt wasn't going to make it through that last squeeze hole." She gave Randy a seductive look.

"That's why I was goosin' you, Babe," Randy snickered. "Well, let's get a hustle on and see what's ahead. I'm hungry as hell. Man, I could sure use a Baby Ruth or a babe of any kind about now." Connie made the echoes replay her laughter many times before Shannon put a playful hand over her mouth.

"Maybe we can find a dryer place," Monty suggested, looking around at the dripping walls and leading the way through a stone arch that led into a much bigger chamber.

"Look how much lighter it is down toward the end," Connie exclaimed. "Betchie we're about to reach the outside." But as they rounded a large column of limestone, they all stopped in shocked silence, shielding their eyes against the brightness of a blazing campfire in the middle of a huge domed room. Around the campfire sat three bearded men, who eyed the newcomers with suspicious eyes.

"I'll be damned," Randy gasped. "If it ain't that Baadshaw bunch from over Jasper way. That one standing in the shadows is Hank Baadshaw."

Shannon recalled her father's story about the draft-dodging Baadshaw clan, how Hank got caught but received a medical discharge from the army after turning to pee into his bunk every morning in basic training. She realized the men all had the lantern-jawed, Neanderthal look of the Baadshaws.

Suddenly, a very tall, bald man stepped out of the darkness of the tunnel and stood watching them inscrutably with his arms folded across the black tunic he wore. His chin thrust forward with horizontal lines emanating from thin lips reminiscent of a baricuda. Sparse chin whiskers followed the line of his neck down to the gray hair showing at the open neck of his Nehru-style coat. The diaper-like loin cloth he wore resembled one Shannon had seen pictured recently on a Sikh warrior in a book about India.

"To whom do we owe the honor of this visit?" his commanding voice asked, as Monty approached cautiously. He fixed Monty with eyes that seemed to reflect the blaze. Then he bowed toward them, revealing a coiled serpent tattooed on his head, and added, "I am MostHi FOU."

Monty stuck out his hand, trying to keep his voice from revealing his nervousness. "Oh, Mr. FOU," he acknowledged awkwardly, not sure of the correct manner of addressing this personage. "I'm Monty Villines, Dallas Villines' son. I grew up around here but don't recall meeting you."

The men said nothing, so Monty nervously introduced Shannon, Connie and Randy. Still Mr. FOU made no attempt to introduce his slack-jawed followers who appeared to be stoned or drunk. So this accounted for the smell of grass, Shannon thought, feeling panicky at thought of what they might have stumbled into. These mountain men have long been associated with moonshining, she remembered.

"Have you explored beyond this point, Sir?" Monty asked.

"Ah, yes. Extensively!" FOU replied, warming long-nailed fingers over the fire. "In fact, we have accumulated extraordinary artifacts, which I might be willing to show you were I convinced you would not reveal our secrets to outsiders. You understand the government would likely confiscate these valuables and remove them from the people in this area: I think the local people should alone profit from these treasures." His stature added to his Sikh likeness, Shannon decided.

"Right, Man!" Randy exclaimed, his eyes glowing at thought of legendary Confederate gold. "We'll do whatever you say!" He rubbed his hands gleefully. "What 'd you find?"

CHAPTER V

Monty still appeared hesitant as Randy attempted to shake hands with FOU. FOU ignored Randy's proffered hand. He kept compelling eyes on Monty and the girls. "Hell, we'll keep our traps shut," declared Randy. "Ask Ole Baadshaw over there. He knows me. You know ole Randy's a man of his word, doncha Hank?" Hank aimed a stream of sputum with his amber-colored lip at the fire and grunted. The stench mixed with that of dampness and stale sweat, bringing cold sweat to Shannon's brow. *Hank has three eyes, her mental computer reported.* She jumped, releasing some of her nervousness, when Connie poked her from where the other girl cowered in her shadow. *The eye in the middle isn't red.*

"I gotta git outa here," Connie whispered. "I'm about to pee my britches." She did a braided-legged dance to demonstrate the urgency. Unaware of how the room magnified sound, she went on. "I ain't kiddin', girl. That weirdo scares the pee outa me! Him an that Baadshaw with the tatooed eye!"

FOU's strange mouth formed into something between a smile and a grimace and he asked, "Perhaps the young ladies would like some privacy?" He bowed toward them, and Shannon observed that what she had taken to be a birthmark in the middle of his forehead was actually a tatooed serpent's tongue. He pointed a yellowish, long finger toward the shadowy recesses where the tunnel exited behind him. "You may retire to the alcove," he suggested, while his hypnotic, dark eyes commanded the girls to leave. As they left, with Connie clenching her heavy legs, his deep voice rolled like thunder in the tomb-like enclosure. "When you return, we shall have tea". He ordered one of the mountain men to draw some water from the well, and place it on the coals to boil. The bearded one left carrying a bucket on a rope.

Later, as FOU served the tea, Shannon stared at the strange seared brands on each of his long-fingered hands. On the left, she saw a puffed,skull-shaped scar; on the right a burned-in design that she recalled from the book about India and Tibet. "What does this brand signify?" she asked as he fixed her with those Charles-Manson-eyes His accent sounds almost English, very clipped, she realized.

"That is a Tibetan motif--the Seven Paths," he replied curtly, moving on and discouraging further questions. He must be nearly eight feet tall, huge, she reasoned as he bent to avoid brushing overhanging stalactites with the spikey tufts of hair on either side of his forehead.

She studied FOU as he went around the firelit circle serving the tea. The long tunic and dhoti-loin-cloth, thong sandals, his stature, and the strangely shaped goatee were those of a Sikh warrior from India. Young Sikh men curled their sprouting beards and pinned them beneath the chin, she had read, in order to comply with their religious edict against cutting the hair. But none had been pictured either bald or with the two strange tufts like those on either side of FOU's forehead; however, they were all wearing turbans, she realized. But what on earth would an Indian Sikh be doing here in this backwoods area of the Ozarks?

"We have sandwiches and fruit we can share with everyone," Randy offered seemingly determined to ingratiate himself in some manner with FOU. But, while the mountain men grabbed most of the sandwiches and apples, wolfing them down, FOU sat cross-legged, sipping his tea and looking into the fire. When not a crumb of food remained, he rose and beckoned them to follow as he lit a kerosene lantern and proceeded through the tunnel opposite the one through which Shannon and her friends had entered.

"I will show you a few samples of the things we have found," FOU promised, after walking a way in total silence.

Oh God, there's no telling where he's taking us, Shannon thought. *We're at their mercy down here.* She found herself praying panicky little petitions as they went further into the mountain.

FOU paused as they encountered another passage, partially closed by a rockfall. "Look at the size of those fallen stalactites and stalagmites," he ordered, holding the light aloft so the vast carnage could be viewed. At that point, Shannon realized that the three mountain men formed an effective blockade, walking shoulder to shoulder behind them, blocking any chance of retreat as FOU led them further and further into the maze. She fought her sense of dread and rising hysteria as FOU's deep voice echoed back from the chamber of carnage. "This occurred before God grew jealous of Lucifer and sent Him to rule the earth." His eyes shining like burning coals in the semi-darkness, he held the lantern over the fallen statuary. "And this occurred eons ago, long before recorded history!" From hooded eyes, he studied their reactions.

"Man, how do you know?" Randy asked, sounding surprised, but without the fear evident on the faces of the other members of his party.

"Because I was here!" MostHi FOU stated matter-of-factly. As Monty and Shannon's mouths dropped open, a cunning look came over the giant guru's face. Then he elbowed Monty and winked at Shannon. "Because I know scientifically how many years it takes dripping water to form those six-foot-stalactites, you oaf!" he said icily to Randy. He flashed that chameleon smile-grimace at Shannon that made her blood flow like crushed ice. When he leaned to stare at her, her heart seemed to freeze for several heartbeats.

"Yow, right-on, Man! This is bullshit!" Randy chuckled, slapping FOU's shoulder playfully. "You think I thought you was here—I know you look old but not *that* old!" Randy flashed a rotten-toothed smile.

"Never touch me again," he said to Randy in a low, menacing tone. Randy shrank like a pricked balloon.

Monty and Shannon exchanged glances that spoke volumes to Shannon about the extent to which Monty shared her feelings.

She reached for his big hand to stop her shaking, feeling as if she might black out from diarrheic surges of fear that left her nauseous and weak.

"Where do you come from originally?" Monty asked their guide. Before answering, FOU hesitated; he walked over and knelt by a shelf of rock. He paused for a few seconds, murmuring some incantation, then answered: "MostHi FOU does not think or talk about His yesterdays, only today." Reaching back under the shelf of limestone, he extracted a human skeleton on a rotting reed pallet. Two tiny ears of corn and some acorns lay in a clay pot beside the gnarled skeletal finger bones.

"My God! Where'd you find that?" gasped Monty, while the girls turned away, exchanging revolted looks.

"Do not be alarmed, ladies," FOU soothed, rising and brushing his hands. "She can't hurt you, Just an Indian squaw who died—oh—probably around the time Columbus came to the new world. " He bent over and gingerly touched the broken pelvic bones of the skeleton,thrusting a finger where the vagina had been with a salacious grin. "Probably died in childbirth," His face hardened, and he seemed to wish to neasure the effect of his words on the girls as his cruel lips parted to reveal small, pointed teeth. "Women have always paid for their pleasure," he chuckled, a sound like ice cubes in a glass.

Shannon shivered as he pushed the grisly remains back out of sight and remarked, "Just an example of the less valuable artifacts I spoke about. I'm sure you've heard of the Civil War treasures rumored to have been hidden here, payrolls for the Confederate armies, et cetera." His strange eyebrows, forming inverted vees, rose almost to the tatooed tongue on his forehead. "They were not rumors," he challenged, daring them to question.

"This is fascinating," Monty said, looking at his watch, "but we must start back now in order to reach the cave entrance by rendezvous time at four o'clock." Shannon felt staggered, too tired to think of the long trek back, yet ready to crawl, if necessary, to escape this threatening situation.

MostHi FOU studied them speculatively. "There is a short-cut nearby which I might show you if you are willing to take a blood oath never to reveal it to anyone else,"

"Hell, Yow! I reckon so!" Randy yodeled. "I'm tard of crawlin thu this here mole hole. Lead us to it, Man! We'll do anything!"

"You mean there's really a shortcut topside?" Monty asked in amazement. "I've lived here all my life. Never heard of such a thing."

"Sure, we were in here long before the entrance clearance," FOU declared. "But each of my witnesses took the blood oath never to reveal this."

"Blood oath," Monty repeated. "Exactly what does that involve?" His eyes revealed concern to Shannon.

"Hellfar", Hank Baadshaw interjected, opening his mouth for the first time except to bolt down food; "hit don't take no blood hardly. Jest scratch yer wrist and mix yer blood. That's it, as a feller says; that's all she wrote." FOU's smouldering eyes studied them, then his bearded followers.

"It involves much more than the simple ceremony. It signifies a solemn vow of silence about this place and everything connected with me. To break this vow will bring instant retribution to you and your families. You will come to realize that MostHi Father of the Universe is all-knowing, all-powerful."

"I'm not sure we will take an oath, but we do promise not to reveal your presence or the mountain exit," Monty offered, looking at the girls, then at FOU.

Connie giggled nervously, pasty as yeast dough."Us girls won't tell!" Salt-rimmed sweaty circles extended from her armpits to elbows. She looked at Shannon pleadingly. "Will we, girl?"

"But, Sir, if we take this here blood oath, can we, like—come back thu this short-cut and explore with you?" Randy's pupils resembled two dollar signs.

"Certainly," FOU agreed. "However, I will never show you the exit or allow you to leave unless you take the blood oath." His menacing manner left no choice, only sinking sensations as the four hostages exchanged glances.

FOU motioned toward the ceiling of the bell-shaped cavern as they entered.

"You notice that this dome is not smoked in spite of the large bonfire? That's because the smoke travels out a fissure in the mountain-top." He added, "Many people around here assume this smoke to be fog on Magic Mountain or a moonshine operation. But the mountain is more magic than these oafs suspect. You've heard hill folk speculate about origin of a skull, even say Skull Cave's tunnels run to Devil's Den over

Harrison way?" FOU made his black eyebrows do a derisive dance below his tatoo. "I knew the owner of that skull!"

"Really?" Monty said, playing for time to decide, "Nobody was missing so locals assumed an animal dragged it from back in the cave, maybe Confederate remains."

"I tell you it belonged to my servant, John Wilkes Booth who rid the world of Abraham Lincoln. I know your history books do not report the disappearance of this trophy, but I was there. You assume it's impossible like most illiterates. You mountaineers have no vision. Nothing is impossible to MostHi FOU!"

Shannon read scepticism and fear as Monty turned to mouth words, "Looks like we have to take the oath to escape." Turning back, he said to FOU: "The others are willing to take the blood oath." He looked at his watch uneasily. "We have to make it fast though or the chaperones will be sending searching parties for us..."

MostHi FOU unpinned a star-shaped pin from his black tunic, and asked Monty to present his wrist. Then FOU scratched himself and mixed their blood. In silence broken only by the dying ember's crackle, FOU then scratched Shannon's wrist, staring into her eyes for long minutes. A chill raced over her; she felt as if her blood coagulated as his icy talon-nails held her shaking arm. Weakness spread over her; she heard raven cries, and began to black out. Falling, she grabbed for support, powerless to stop, grasping FOU's dhoti.

"A-h-h, so!" FOU crooned, looking down at her. "See how she swoons and reaches for me!" He pulled her close, so that she felt his hardness. "Already trying to undress me." He pulled his loin cloth higher.

Monty pushed him away angrily and held the shaking girl at his side as FOU administered the oath to Connie and Randy. FOU's cruel mouth snapped shut, and he glared at Monty.

"Are you able to walk?" Monty asked with a concerned look at Shannon. "You're white as a sheet."

As she nodded, Randy agreed that both girls looked "white as sheep, alright!"

Hank Baadshaw's whitish-blue eyes looked down his toucan-bill nose at Shannon. "You gonna feel power like you ain't never knowed," he hissed.

Shannon shivered, hoping the evil smelling hulk could not read her mind. *He looks nearly blind, with the eyes of a shedding snake. I wonder if that tatooed eye is some sight-restoring ritual. He's like those blind fish, underground so long he's losing his sight. No wonder he's looking for a father, anyone to support him.*

CHAPTER VI

Monty and his group followed silently as FOU led then back in the direction from which they had first entered his council chamber. Stopping near the arch, he gestured to his bearded cohorts toward a large boulder. Without a word, the mountain men put their shoulders to the stone, began to rock it, grunting mightily from their efforts. Jed ripped the galluses from his faded overalls. As the trousers dropped, revealing his bare, hairy haunches before he could turn loose of the boulder, the others roared with laughter. Covering his privates with a large hand, the mountaineer grabbed his fallen apparel with the other hand and ran off awkwardly, unable to extract his high-topped brogans from the overalls.

"Easy to see ole Baadshaw hangs out with the men instead of the boys!" shouted Randy, laughing raucously and slapping his leg."Ole Jed can't even pull his own britches up. An Jed's the smart one!"

FOU did not smile, although he watched Jed Baadshaw's ignominius retreat toward the council chamber. Turning back toward Monty and the girls, he fixed large, dark eyes on their faces. Then he placed both hands between his eyes with the fingertips touching the snake tatoo at his hairline.

"Salaam, Sahib and Memsahibs," he intoned solemnly. "Never forget your blood vow to MostHi FOU for a moment lest you pay with the rest of your blood." With this chilling farewell, he watched until Randy followed the others up the stone steps behind the boulder.

At the end of the short stairway, they found themselves inside an old well or cistern that had been lined with fieldstone. Zigzaged up the side of the well were rock projections barely large enough to hold a human foot. Dripping water and moss, this means of escape looked slippery and extremely dangerous in the semi-darkness, lighted only by a crack of light through the boards covering the old well. About three feet below the level on which the group stood, a snake swam lazy circles in the dark waters.

Looking at the snaky waters and then lifting frightened eyes to the slimy stepping stones above, Shannon wailed: "Oh God, FOU knows we can't climb this without falling. He's probably waiting in there to enjoy our last screams!" Once again, she felt her emotions going out of control. The well repeated her warnings eerily.

"Worse'n that," Randy cackled, "he probly got the water to make that tea outa this here well."

"Be serious, Randy," Monty said angrily. "More than likely, if he doesn't hear us fall, he'll send the Baadshaws out here to throw us in."

"Aw, he ain't gonna ruin his water supply with the likes of us," Randy smirked. "You're takin' that weird dude too serious. He's plumb fulla shit!"

Shannon's legs began to quiver visibly and she could not control the shivers that ran over her body. "I'm sorry," she said, "I just about lost it in there, and I'm still feeling really nauseated."

Monty pulled her to his side. "You're just exhausted," he said gently, holding the quivering girl close. "We'll rest a minute and think positive. If we only concentrate on taking one step at a time up that well, we'll be up on the mountain top in a few minutes. O. K., Shanny?" He stretched his long leg up to the first projection, "I'm taking the first step and raking that ooze off with my boot so it won't be so slippery. Then, give me your hand and I'll pull you up behind me. " He tested the nearest rock which dislodged under his weight and fell with a terrific splash that threw more moisture on them and the nearby stones. Their eyes locked during a terrified silence. Both drew strength from the sense of connection.

"That probably wasn't meant to be a step," he said to reassure the panicky girls. Reaching to one side, he used his hands to clear a mossy rock for a handhold: Then he planted his boot on the next step and tested it before risking his full weight. It held and he reached for Shannon, wondering how the shaking legs of this fragile-looking girl could possibly stretch so far, praying as he grabbed her icy hand and almost lifted her bodily.

He held her until the shaking stopped and almost had to peel her loose to go further.

"Man, this is where we really test the strength of this step," said Randy as he reached the first foothold and leaned over to help Connie up. Connie's face looked cottony against the darkness of the water below, but she still managed to smile weakly at Randy's cruel humor. "Think light, Lotta Momma," he grunted as he hefted her weight.

After what seemed an eternity, Monty lifted Shannon to the stone cap around the well's top. He had pushed the weathered oak cover off with his head and still had some of the slimy moss shining atop his dark head. His western shirt welded to his muscular body from exertion and stress.

They hugged each other ecstatically, breathing deeply of the spring breeze, glorying in the feel of the sun on their icy bodies. "Thank God, we made it; we made it!" she exulted before she collapsed on a huge slab of limestone covered with lichen rosettes, totally spent.

Looking up at Monty with misty eyes, she said in a choking voice, "I'd never have gotten out of there without you. Are you sure that isn't a halo you're wearing?" She touched the ring of damp moss on his head.

"Not hardly," he said, grinning as he pulled it out of his hair. "Lordy, that was scary. Thank God we're safe." He gave her an intense soul-stirring look.

As soon as Randy helped the panting Connie to the surface, Monty closed the well cover and went to determine the direction of the cave entrance. In a few minutes, Monty shouted back to the girls:

"Guess what, we're on Skull Bluff right above the farmhouse. Can you believe it?" He hurried back to them, looking surprised and jubilant. "I can't believe it; we can make it back in plenty of time for the rendezvous and no questions asked."

Shannon's eyes searched Monty's face before she asked incredulously, "You mean we're really not going to tell anyone about what that weirdo is doing?"

"Course not!" Randy declared promptly. "We'd have to be idiots to give up a chance to get rich. Probly only chance guys like us will ever see."

"I haven't really thought it through," Monty said, avoiding her eyes.

"What's to think through?" Randy snorted. "Me - I've heard all my life how them rebels hid their entire treasury in this cave. Nobody could git in to check 'er out. Why you think Ole Fooey don't want us to tell anybody about it? Not 'cause he's savin' it for us local yokels; you can bet a pritty on that. He plans to steal it 'fore anybody gits a chanct to see it."

"But what if this is a drug operation, or something even more sinister?" Shannon asked. "That man has an evil presence; I can't explain it. Didn't you feel it, Connie?" Everyone except Randy still appeared fearful,but Connie donned a cheerful expression as Randy's pale eyes swiveled her way.

"Aw, I've seen my daddy act worse," she chuckled. She snuggled close to Smith.

"We did take a vow of secrecy," Monty said slowly, surprising himself almost as much as he did Shannon with his reluctance. His gaze dropped before her directness and he drew circles in the dirt with his cowboy boot. "I don't know; I just don't feel good about taking that oath and breaking my word..."

Randy's small eyes grew as he speculated about what the cave might hold. His voice rose shrilly.

"Man, we might get enough gold outa there to never have to work a'gin. An' all the papers be writin' about the arty facts we haul outa there. Hellfar, we'd be famous too overnight."

"You mean you ain't afraid to go back in there?" Connie asked, looking at Randy worshipfully as he pranced around with his nose in the air. His greasy hair had escaped its rubber band to hang down his back.

"H-e-l-l no!" he boasted. "I seen a lotta mystics like Ole Fooie in Nam. Messed up on drugs. Why, we had a lotta niggers thought they was Mohammed. One even changed his name from Sylvanus Jonas Smith to `Mohammed Ben Scrood." He laughed and slapped his knee. "I was glad `cause the guys quit astin me if he was my brother."

"I think the man is capable of murder if we break our vow," Monty said with deep conviction. "I'm just not willing to take the risk while we're all here close and so vulnerable. He may have access to every one of those tunnels in Skull Cave for all we know.

I want to know more about him before I take the risk. O.K.?" The girls stared back, big-eyed as owls.

"Hellfar, I'll break my vow to that geek when I get good an ready" said Randy, "Mr. High 'n Mighty Monty. You ain't my boss." He gave Monty his Humphrey Bogart look, obviously to impress Connie. "Right now, I aim to cooperate with FOU until I see which way the trade winds blow. In fact, I'm planning to go back in there tonight." He whipped out a cigarette and offered Connie one.

"I hear the wind blowing, Randy, but it isn't the trade winds," Monty said angrily. "You're even crazier than I think if you go back into that place." He gathered his gear and motioned to the rest to follow. "I thank God we got out at all!"

"He don't scare me either," Connie announced, linking her arm with Randy's, puffing a cigarette.

After negotiating the house size boulders that led down to the farmhouse, Monty tired of Randy's boasting. He said grimly, "Quit blowin' smoke, Smith. Let's meet the others, keep our mouths shut and get some rest."

"Great idea," Shannon agreed. "I'll never forget MostHi FOU as long as I live, or this day. But I hope I never live long enough to see him again." She shivered in spite of the rays of setting sun.

"Don't worry, Red, you won't if you break that blood oath!" Randy jeered.

Monty added soberly: "To be on the safe side, let's play it cool. Remember, the rest of you will be going back to Kingsville on the other side of the mountain, but ole Monty's got to live here. 'Live' I said; that's the key word. O.K.?" When Randy argued, he added firmly, "FOU did threaten our families too, you know, and my family and yours could be sitting ducks for this nut."

They all nodded as they rose and headed for the rendezvous.

CHAPTER VII

After joining the other explorers, complaining along with them of nothing more eventful than sprains from falls, exhaustion and sore muscles, Monty's group gathered back at the farmhouse. When darkness began to shadow the cove, Monty asked Shannon to help him gather wood for the fireplace. As they strolled to the edge of the woodland, he took her hand and said, "Sweet Shanny, doesn't twilight-time yesterday seem a world away from now? I felt as close to you last evening as I thought possible with another human being—let alone a woman. But, I feel even closer tonight and in a different way."

"I know," she murmured. "I'll never forget what we shared today—ever. Even in this peaceful place, listening to the whip-poorwills. I can scarcely shake that feeling of impending doom. Or that ghoulish guru's evil spell! His eyes haunt me!"

He stopped and grasped her shoulders, looking deep into her eyes. "You felt that too? My dad's always been so spooked by the unseen that I thought maybe it was genetic. That I was imagining the evil aura." She snuggled closer.

"Did you feel a chill when FOU mixed your blood with his?" She shivered, then looked at her arms as they responded to the memory with goose bumps. "The way my hair felt, I think it must have stood at attention."

He ran his fingers through her hair, pretending pricks on his fingers, obviously glorying in what he saw and felt.

"Me too," he agreed. "I reckon I'm just a superstitious hillbilly, but I still can't bring myself to break that stupid vow." He winced. "I still see his sadistic face, feel his power for evil.."

"I know. Something about his eyes reminds me of that guy that killed Sharon Tate in California. So brutal! Whatsis face? Um, oh, Charles Manson."

"Exactly!" he exclaimed triumphantly. "Maniac eyes. That's who I thought of too." He did a double-take at her. "Amazing how our minds run in the same. . . "

"Yes, in the same channel," she said simultaneously. "Another case of great minds running in the same channel." They both laughed exultantly and he pulled her close against his body in the shadow of a huge Elm. For a moment, Shannon yearned for his kiss. As he stood looking down at her, every fiber of her being hungered for him. Sorry that his better judgment had overruled the hunger in his dark eyes, as he released her, she knew he had felt her over-powering desire through her trembling.

He sank down on an ivy-covered log and pulled her down beside him.

"I was sorry you heard the rukus between Connie and Missy," he began, fanning himself with his stetson. "I know Missy is a bit jealous."

Shannon fought for control, return of her common sense. "Well, I didn't know, but I do now. As I told you, Dad didn't want me in the play let alone on this trip. But there's always been this silly rivalry between town girls like Missy and farm girls like me. Even more so with girls from the mountains like Connie. I suppose there's always people who only feel better if they find someone to look down on."

"Really ridiculous," he said gruffly. "I don't understand it at all. Same thing with Randy and black people."

"I think so too, probably because of my folks' attitudes. Mama always said my dad didn't feel better than anyone—but every bit as good. Mama Josie says if my daddy met the President, he'd poke out a big hand with mechanic grease stains in the cracks and never hesitate. He would too!"

"Sounds like my dad," Monty agreed. "Just one difference, Ole Dallas Villines ain't afraid of no man, but he does look down on anybody who is."

"He'd have been proud of you today with Ole FOU."

"I'm not so sure. He would probably have marched outa there and called the Law. I don't think he ever forgave me for being scared of dogs after I got bitten by a pit-bulldog as a little tyke."

"You don't think he would have been scared of old FOU?"

"Maybe," he said thoughtfully. "He's always had this thing about something he can't see. Never would go in Skull Cave. Oh, he'd never admit it, but he would never go over in Booger Holler back of our place either at night. He might pick up on FOU's invisible evil."

"I thought maybe you were afraid of Missy," she teased, "but not because she's a dog."

"Maybe, a little," he said to her surprise. "Women totally mystify me—especially girls like Missy that like to play manipulations games. They seem to speak a different language. Maybe if I had sisters..."

"I really don't understand most other women myself," she admitted. "Maybe because I grew up almost entirely with boys. Even now, I usually never see girls in summer except at church.

I've always hunted, fished and swam with my brothers. As a result, Mama says I'm too direct, talk like a field hand sometimes." She watched closely to see if he appeared to agree.

"Yes, you are direct like a guy. But these women who set man-traps scare the hell outa me. I don't think I'm stupid enough to get caught but—well, I don't seem to speak the same language. What else can I tell you?"

He made a helpless gesture with his big hands. She wondered if he thought of Missy. "Most men and women do speak a different language" she agreed. "I guess it wouldn't matter if we didn't need each other to be complete."

"I hope you're speaking about us specifically," he teased, making her blush.

"Well, I heard you warn Randy about jail bait," she reminded. "Was that based on a past experience of yours?"

"Oh, no," he said, looking embarrassed. "I just know how ole Randy thinks."

"I know. Makes me furious the way he treats Connie. But she won't listen. Poor girl has probably never had a date; she's just so vulnerable."

"I hate that Missy humiliated her before everyone," he said sympathetically. "Poor kid has had way too much of that already. When she was about thirteen, I saw her once trying to get her father into his pickup at that little country store at Red Star. He was drunk, calling her awful names. A bunch of people were gawking. He pushed her over from behind the wheel, jumped in and went roaring off down that narrow, steep road. Poor Connie looked like she hoped he would kill both of them. I can still see that tearful face. She was a pretty girl back then before she got so heavy."

"I'd probably build myself a fort of fat if I were Connie, too," she surmised. "I'm afraid she still wants to die most of the time in spite of that cheerful mask she wears." He nodded sadly.

CHAPTER VIII

"Them stars look dang near close enough to touch," Randy Smith said, looking at them reflected in Connie's eyes, "don't they, Baby?"

"I think I did touch them when we were making love!" she whispered as they lay in the grass between two limestone pyramids close to the old well on Magic Mountain. "What a night! I'm still so excited I could just die," she panted, struggling from beneath his weight to gasp for air.

"Like WOW, baby!" Randy chortled, admiring her nude body in the bright moonlight. He reached over to cuddle her large breasts. "I ain't been with a chick like you since my hippie days in L.A! Ain't hardly any gals in these hills brave enough to make out on a mountain top. I knew the first time I saw you that you was for me." He gave her another probing kiss.

"My old man ain't afraid of the Devil hisself. Reckon I'm a little like him?" She stared at the night sky, sobered by the thought of her father. "Aren't you really a little bit afraid of FOU, Randy? He spooks me out to the max."

"Hell, no. I got ole Hank to take me to pee and ast him about FOU. Says FOU claims he's the Father of the Universe, that's where his name comes from. Crazy as a Bessie Bug, I think. Betchie he ain't even from India. I seen a lot like him in 'Nam. Some of our guys turnt a yaller color from taking Atabrine for malaria, even had their eyes slanted. Pretended to be Oriental like ole Buddha, fat bellies an all! Most weirded out from drugs an lost touch with the fact they was just ole Joe Blow from Idaho."

"But FOU's eyes, the way they stare right into my lost soul. Sort've bend my mind. Know what I mean?" Randy jumped astride of her and stared into her eyes, pulling his hair up in tufts on either side of his head.

"You mean like this, Baby Doll?" he clowned. "Surely, you don't believe that phoney baloney Most-High-Father-of-the Universe stuff. I know you aint ever been outa Arkansas but you ain't ignorant an stupid, are you?"

"I've probably seen the Devil up close a lot more'n you have," she said, fighting tears. "When my daddy gets to drinking, he can shame the Devil with meanness he conjures up. FOU, he seems real to me! I'll tell you the truth, I'm scared to go back in there."

"Aw, now, don't start actin' like some dumb woman on me! Hellfar, we stand to be rich if we don't chicken out here. That weirdo ain't no Father of Humanity. FOU ain't the father of nuthin but lies."

"Well, I guess you're right. Nothing risked, nothing gained. An I reckon he couldn't do anything to me my own father ain't already done. You got no idea how many times I seen the Devil up close in my daddy an my sorry brothers."

"I may have to beat the crap outa your old man an them stupid brothers of yours when this is over an git you outa that mess!" he boasted.

Self-conscious in her nudity, Connie grabbed her tee shirt that read "Kingsville Queens, Kingsville, Arkansas," As she struggled to get her sweaty torso into it, Randy grabbed her shorts and panties and hoisted them high on a stick.

,"We'll use this for our flag as we storm the hide-out of MostHi FOU!" he roared. "If that one's father of the Universe, I'm a nigger aviator. I think a rabid bat bit him. Or else he was born John Doe and a brick shy of a load." He gestapo-stepped toward the old well with the flag.

Connie shielded her privates with a puffy hand. "That's what scares me," she admitted, shivering in spite of the warm night. She hugged her breasts so hard that they mounded above the low-cut shirt. "Crazy people do crazy, cruel things to other people. My daddy's crazy as a loon from drinking so much, and you probably wouldn't believe the things he does. Why, he even ties me up and does awful, cruel, unnatural things to me."

"I know," Randy said, trying his best to look sympathetic but unable to kill the lust in his pale eyes. "Your brothers told us about it onct at school."

"You promise you'll kill all of them for me?" she asked. "I'd help you. We could do anything together." Connie's voice turned gutteral as she swore "sons a bitches. I'd like to gut em like fattenin'hogs!"

"Sure we can. An you got no call to be afraid tonight. I got a knife in my boot if things go wrong. But ole FOU did invite us to come back. Would he have done that an not killed us while we were down there if he meant us any harm?" He undid his ponytail, shook it loose, then finger-combed it.

"But what do you think he wants with us? We got no money or anything."

"I think he may have a drug operation going back in there. Maybe cookin' up batches of LSD. I know he's got great pot, cause ole Hank gave me a drag of weed after we peed. But, whatever, he needs some smarter contact than that Baadshaw bunch. Which means yours truly could be the pipeline for a lotta moolah." His eyes glittered. "Stick with me, baby, an I'll show you the world!" After binding his hair back with a rubber band, he retrieved his flag. He untied her clothing from the flagpole and handed it to her. She still eyed him hesitantly, as he snapped his fingers and urged her to get ready to make the descent through the well "FOU's just a legend in his own mind'" he said.

"Blows my mind just to climb down over that snaky water," she said tremulously. She ended up with both legs inside one of the large shorts.

"But just think how you're going to spend that rebel gold that's been hidden in there. An we'll show up that smart-ass Missy, when you're driving around in a cool car in diamonds and furs. We'll show them we're not stupid clods."

She struggled to extract sweaty thighs, grunting. "You sure you're not just actin' brave..." Finally, she donned the shorts, still eying him questioningly.

"Woman, you oughta know better'n anybody ole Randy got plenty of balls!" She formed an "O" with forefinger and thumb, as he went on. "Speakin' of balls, Ole Hank is the one freaks me out. He's got a metal earring thu his dong! I ain't bullin', woman! He showed me when he was peein'. Lookin' at me with them three eyes!"Randy snorted with laughter, erasing the creases in his cheeks for a moment.

Her tremulous soprano queried "You understand I ain't had cause to trust any men?" Is he using me too, Connie questioned herself.

"Yow, but maybe that's why you got this adventurous spirit. I ain't never seen no woman that would do what you already done tonight. Sneakin' out with me right under the noses of them ole biddies. Makin whoopie with me right out under the stars. Something I always dreamed about. But even in my dreams, even the wet ones, it wasn't as good as you, Babe."

"You really think so," she asked, feeling doubtful still of his sincerity.

"You better believe it. How'd you git so good? Virgins usually ain't worth a hoot. I reckon yore daddy an brothers served some good purpose with their ornery ways." Looking offended, she frowned even when he hugged her. She sank down on one of the lichen covered boulders, looking dejected.

"I ain't goin' a step if you talk about them," she threatened.

"You do this with me, hon, and you can be mine forever," he promised, putting his arms around her. Then he French-kissed her.

"You promise you'll protect me, whatever happens?" she panted.

"Sure, and we can do what we done earlier at least onct a day." She rose and he led her to the well. "Here goes for the biggest adventure of our lives!" he promised. "But watch as you climb down. Them steps may be slick as owl shit."

After Randy's first step down the well, Connie watched, feeling she must have lost her mind to be following him. His face looked pale and wide-eyed as he stared up at her. She could see the moon reflected in the water and ripples where the snake still swam there.

"Can't we wait for daylight?" she pleaded. "I don't think I can..."

"Come on now or lose your one chanct for a life," he insisted. "Wanta settle for being a fat ole maid slave to a buncha drunks?" She hoisted one heavy leg over the well-curb, then did a belly-buster, feeling for the step.

CHAPTER IX

Once they entered the cave, Randy turned on his flashlight and stood listening. The stillness seemed as absolute as had the darkness.

"Reminds me of a tomb," Connie whispered. "Oh, God, why'd I say that? Or even think about that," she quavered, finding some reassurance in hearing her own voice.

"They probly went somers," Randy conjectured, making his light do an eerie march along the floor and dripping walls. He kicked the charcoaled limbs remaining from the previous day's fire. "Been gone almost as long as we have." Eyes glistening with greed, he proposed "Let's see if we can find the loot an bug outa here before they come back!"

Connie grasped his shirttail as he proceeded down the tunnel toward the area where the skeleton had been displayed by FOU. Through chattering teeth, she asked, "You ain't going to take that skeleton, are you?"

"Naw, that's probly valuable to some museum, but nuthin' compared with what I hope to find. Gonna git us gold, Baby."

Suddenly, Randy halted, looking back at her with his finger to his lips. "Uh-oh," he whispered. "Think I hear somebody comin'."

To Connie's nervous perusal, he looked scared, and she wondered if his bravado had all been a part of his macho posing. To her horror, he pulled her to the shelf of rock where the Indian skeleton had been hidden and commanded that she roll underneath while he secreted himself behind a tall limestone column nearby. He pulled the knife from his boot and doused the light.

As the footsteps came closer, Connie stage whispered, holding herself: "I'm just about to pee my britches, Randy. If I touch that skeleton, I'll roll outa here, peein' down my legs and squalling like a baby."

"You better not, Sweet Pea! Not if you don't want Ole FOU to put a plug in you." She heard his nervous twitching as he warned her to be still and stay hidden until he sized up their situation.

The booted feet approached closer, sending ominous rumbles echoing through the tunnel. Connie forced the screams to die in her throat as she had learned to do early in life. From the sound, she decided some heavy object was being dragged along the limestone floor of the tunnel. She could tell that the men stopped to rest every few steps and soon recognized the voices of the Baadshaws. Animalistic grunts accompanied every exertion.

"Git a fire goin', boys," ordered Hank's rough voice, and she could hear them breaking branches, then the crackle of flames. As the fire lit up the cavern, she hugged the musty wall, afraid the mountaineers might bend and spy her under the limestone shelf which barely covered her bulk. She also spied the old reed mat only a foot away from her head and fancied she could even smell its occupant, As MostHi FOU's icy comment sneaked into her memory filling her with terror, she tried to close her mind to the words: "Women have always had to pay for their pleasure." *Am I about to pay for my pleasure now with Randy?* Guilt and fear made her want to writhe in agony, but she dared scarcely breathe.

Then she heard the approach of authoritive footsteps and MostHi FOU's voice inquiring: "Did you find the sacrifice I requested?"

"Oh God, that's a body they just dragged in," she whispered peeking out in spite of her fear. By the fire with its legs extended grotesquely lay a large bull calf, which the Baadshaws were dragging from the shadows for FOU's inspection. FOU watched inscrutably, his cruel mouth grim.

"He got some great balls on him," Hank Baadshaw boasted, spitting at a coffee can near the fire. He lifted them for FOU's inspection, with a snaggled ear-to-ear grin.

MostHi FOU nodded and handed Hank a scimitar shaped knife. "Proceed with the sacrificial ceremony," he directed, sinking down by the fire,muttering and bowing low seven times. He rose and watched as the Baadshaws severed the bull's testicles, then placed an urn under the animal to catch the spurting blood. Hank's tatooed eye peered through a splatter of blood, but he kept a slack-mouthed smile.

To her amazement, Randy stepped out into the light. He had put away his knife and put on a subservient air. Bowing low before MostHi FOU, he said: "MostHi Father of Humanity, Your obedient servant has returned according to your kind invitation." His hand made a strange rolling motion from his forehead toward his heart as he added: "RomRom Alechum." Clasping hands, he salaamed.

"It's not Father of Humanity," Hank Baadshaw corrected as FOU pinned Randy down with contemptuous eyes. "It's Father of the Universe."

"Oh, pardon my ignorance," Randy said, looking frightened, salaaming again.

"What about the others?" FOU inquired. "Did they spurn my offer?"

"No, Connie came with me," he motioned to where she lay hidden, biting his lip, scuffing the floor nervously. She got her shorts disentangled from a stone spur and rolled out from under the low shelf. "The others hope to come later wh--when they can get away without causing any suspicions."

Now MostHi FOU focused those disconcerting orbs on Connie who did a nervous dance in lieu of holding her privates. "We didn't tell no one, "she blurted. "Um—M—May I please be excused?" She blinked like a cowed child. When he motioned to give her leave, she still could not move. She felt quick-frozen by the image.

Now, he wore a dark hood with a long cape. His face was not covered, and the strange tufts of hair noticeable before near his hairline, stood erect through holes in the head covering. Facing the flames he passed his long fingers through and over them starting a psychedelic light show in the cavern. First, the room filled with fast-moving irridescent shades of green; even the Baadshaws and Randy looked green. Then magenta shaded to deepest purple. His deep voice boomed out of the darkness: "You are just in time to join in our worship ceremony and feast." He bowed deeply toward them and then toward the carcass that seemed spotlighted for a moment as one of the Baadshaws speared the testicles on a three-pronged spit and presented them before MostHi FOU. FOU bowed once more, and the mountain man held the meat over the glowing coals. "To Manhood," growled FOU.

Connie's eyes followed the trail of blood queasily where the bull had been dragged into the cavern. She became even more nauseated when the Baadshaws began to gobble the raw testicles greedily, racing to see which one could devour the most. Randy appeared awe-stricken at the proceedings.

MostHi FOU seemed to read her thoughts as he studied her face.

"Do not be alarmed," he counseled, bringing her a goblet of what appeared to be wine. Too fearful to ask what the glass contained, she began to drink the warm liquid. His eyes willed her to drain every drop and his hypnotic voice urged, "Drink every drop, little one. You will feel more powerful than you have ever felt in your life. This is the nectar prepared by God for his angels, but denied to ordinary women and men. You will never be an ordinary mortal again." She drained the glass.

MostHi FOU lifted the pitcher containing the blood from the bull and served a goblet to each of the men. Pouring himself one, he held it aloft with the toast: "To manhood known only to

Lucifer. To the one we worship and honor above all others in Heaven or on earth." They all joined in the toast solemnly, draining their glasses. Randy threw his to the ceiling with a rebel yell, while the mountain men began cavorting crazily ,giving Connie lascivious looks. Connie forgot her need to go to the alcove as Hank Baadshaw leered at her and confided to Randy: "MostHi FOU always let us use his woman when he through." Gagging, Connie thought: *Hank's gray-blue pupils look like swollen dog ticks.*

Before the taste of the liquid had left Connie's palate, her head began to spin like the whirling lights on the ceiling. Lightning-like traceries of fire flashed over her body activating every sense to a fever pitch. For the first time, she knew the exhiliration of being desired by many men. Staggering, she fell to the floor in the firelight filled with incredible sexual excitement and desire. Continuous orgasms contorted her body into pelvic thrusts toward MostHi FOU. He moved astride her with flames leaping higher in his eyes as the bonfire roared and leaped toward the mind-altering overhead light display. Bats, disturbed by the heat and lights, began circling lower with terrorized cries, their wings beating a rhythm to Connie's orgasmic thrusts.

Above this mind-bending phenomena, Connie heard MostHi FOU's voice, enhanced by the cavernous acoustics.

"You have shared the sacrament of blood with the Great Dragon, the Most High Father of Humanity, the Lovely Lucifer," the voice thundered.

Feeling unbearable animal heat, she tore the clothing from her body and tossed it in the air. Her shorts landed on the bonfire, causing the towering flames to singe many of the bats. As the helpless creatures fell into the inferno, she howled with glee along with the mountain men. A part of her watched this wanton in disbelief while the freed woman gloried in the thought that blossomed in her mind: My father will never enslave me again. *I am indentured to one far more powerful than that drunk who made my flesh crawl as a child.* He will give me everything I desire in this earth if I serve him." Rising, she bowed to kiss his feet, then fell back spread eagled before him, "Take me; oh please take me," she pleaded.

She watched with awe as his member extended until it broke

the loin cloth and the shadow fell across her body. Dimly, she heard Randy's exclamation of surprise. "God damn! A dick with flame throwin dragon. I need me one of them! Hot Damn!"

MostHi FOU towered over the girl, framed by the rearing holocaust as he slowly removed his cape and stroked the dragon. His voice confirmed what her mind had spoken: "I am now your father and your lover. The Father of Ubiquity, MostHi Father of the Universe, the Great Dragon who will now enter your loins to help you praise the lovely Lucifer."

Involuntarily, her face rose to kiss the dragon and allow its tongue of flame to enter her mouth. Then she fell back and felt no pain when the metallic tongue of flame entered her. They writhed around the fire intertwined while Randy and the mountain men watched, shedding their clothing and dancing around them, stroking themselves, begging greedily for turns.

Then MostHi FOU's voice thundered in the rotunda above as he withdrew and rose, looking down at her with those spellbinding eyes:

"You are now one with the Great Dragon, bride of the Lovely Lucifer. You will never again feel unwanted by men."

CHAPTER X

After a drugged sleep, Randy awakened in the cave to the sound of Connie's lusty snoring. Sitting up, he groggily rubbed his gritty face and surveyed the scene of last night's orgy. Totally nude, Connie sprawled with arms and legs akimbo, her fleshy body dimpled in all the wrong places. As Randy stood over her with a feeling of distaste, he noticed a spot of blood on the blanket beneath her hips. The spot had turned dark and dried, so he knew it came from last night's group activities. How'd I ever git so worked up over that, he asked himself, looking at her fleshy lumps with distaste. Her upper arms hung in globules of fat to the elbows. Varicose veins resembled a road map of the rough route her porcine body had known.

"I guess I oughta be sure she ain't half dead," he grumbled, shaking her, but she fell back, limp as a rag doll, continuing to snore. Rummaging around in the alcove, he found some burlap

52

bags and covered her with them, more out of concern for his own comfort than hers. Now what in hell am I going to do, he thought. *Here I am stuck with this spaced-out-broad. If I find the treasure before that bunch gets back, I'd have to leave her here. How'd I ever explain that to her ole man and them wild brothers of hers. They'd as soon shoot me as look at me.*

He poked around the area, trying to locate the treasure in case an opportunity to steal it presented itself. He tore into a trussed up bundle wrapped in a tarppaulin, only to discover the beef hide. Listening to the rumblings of his stomach, he tried to find where the beef had been cached, but there was no trace of it, other than a gristle from one of the testicles. This lay on the dirty floor beside the dead embers of last night's bonfire. Holding his aching head, he slumped down on the shelf near the hiding place of the skeleton, grumbling "Damn, my head don't feel like it'd fit in a washtub. Even my hair is sore. Ole Hank told me FOU gave Connie Spanish Fly among other things, but I'm wonderin' what was in my drinks." Although, Randy had heard no approaching footsteps, suddenly a pair of heavy brogans appeared in his line of vision.

Raising his head so suddenly that he gasped with pain, he looked into the three eyes of Hank Baadshaw. Hank's real eyes look almost blind, he realized.

"Hellfar, scare a man to death!" Randy squalled. "Where you been?"

Hank shuffled around sullenly and said nothing until after he had picked up the tarp-wrapped bundle. "Gotta burn the evidence," he muttered, looking foggy-haired and debauched as Randy felt.

Randy squalled out so irritably that Connie stirred.

"I'm starvin', Man. What tima day is it anyhow?"

"After noon, I reckon." The huge hillbilly started to shuffle away, half-dragging the heavy hide. Noting his massive jaws, Randy recalled his nickname from grade school: "Lantern Jaw". But an upsetting idea squelched his smile.

"OhmiGod! Am I gonna be in trouble! They're probly tearin' up ole Jake back at the Edmonson farmhouse lookin' for us. They'll have the Law after me—or even worse—Connie's brothers." He fought temptation to say "LanternJaw."

"No, they ain't. MostHi FOU had me leave 'em a note 'fore daybreak from Connie sayin' you two had runned off to git married," LanternJaw Baadshaw said.

"But—but—you don't understand. Connie's daddy hates my guts. He'll have my ass for shore!"

"You kiddin? Her ole paw ain't nuthin but a drunk. Been usin' her hisself ever since her maw died."

"How do you know?" Randy asked, feeling distracted by the tatooed eye in the middle of Hank's low forehead. *The man smelled gamey as a billy-goat.*

"Cause I took him some 'shine onct an we pulled a real backwoods bender, me 'n him--an Connie. She was just a kid, but he strung her up in these here handcuff thangs. 'Nuff to make a dog puke. I left!"

"Yow, yow, easy to see yore a real sensitive guy," Randy jeered. "But in the meantime, how am I gonna take care of Connie any better than her ole daddy done. I ain't got a pot to pee in, myself."

Hank stared at him as if his words penetrated very slowly. Shaking his wooly head, he scratched his privates and seemed to be trying to concentrate.

"You don't git it do you, Man?" he muttered. "After you take the sacrament of the Great Dragon, you belong to MostHi FOU. You mix yore blood with his'n. Now he take care of you like he do us ever since we done it."

"What do you mean 'take care of me'? He probably will take care of us like the Mafia does if we don't become his slaves. That what you mean?"

"Why, Man, I don't know about that 'cause I do what he tells me. But he better to me than my ole paw ever was. He gonna give us money, pot an' L.S.D. Helluva lot more than my moonshiner paw ever gived me."

Randy shook his head, groaned and fell down on the blanket beside Connie as the mountain man left with the bull's hide.

CHAPTER XI

As Shannon prepared for breakfast the morning after her

encounter with MostHi FOU, she assumed Connie had gone to the outhouse with some of the other girls. Melissa Evans lolled on the bed in the other bedroom reading a True Story magazine, obviously sulking and planning to stay at the farmhouse when the others left. Just as Shannon reached the kitchen, Miss Cobb burst through the door with her eyes standing out on stems and waving a piece of paper.

"Lookit what we found nailed to the outhouse door!" she yelled. "Does any one know anything about this?" They all looked at each other blankly, except Mrs. Edmonson, who grabbed a potholder to remove a huge iron skillet of scrambled eggs from the Coleman camp stove. "What? What is it?" she asked, wiping her hands on her print apron, obviously finding Miss Cobb's anxiety contagious. She tried to peer around Miss Cobb to read the note.

Miss Cobb adjusted her glasses from where her run had lodged them at the tip of her nose and began to read. Her adenoidal delivery while reading from the shaking paper, coupled with her state of excitement, rendered her announcement almost unintelligible.

"Randy Smith and I decided to quit school and get married, so we are leaving tonight before my daddy can interfere. Tell my ole man he's just lucky I left him alive. Connie Coger Smith"

Miss Cobb read the letter over again to herself, then her mouth dropped open as if the message had just reached her brain: "Randy and Connie eloped last night." She began to wring her hands. "What'll her dad do to us? We were supposed to chaperone her at all times. Her father is violent! Went to jail once for killing his friend in a brawl."

"They done what?" asked the bus driver, looking more puzzled than astounded. As Miss Cobb ignored his question, wailing about her fate to the other teacher, he grumbled, "Lord knows what that stupid Randy might do next. Never had the sense God give a goose even before he went to Viet Nam."

"They eloped, ran off to get married," Miss Cobb said precisely to Gus, still the English teacher in spite of her state of shock.

"Well, if that don't beat a hen a-peckin with a wooden pecker," Gus exclaimed. "Good riddance, I'd say. That's what I'd say to both of them." He stroked his droopy, tobacco-stained handlebar mustache.

Miss Cobb looked the note over once again, mouthing the words. Suddenly, she did a double-take at the scrawled writing. "Why, this isn't Connie's writing! Not her signature either. She always does those fancy curlicues even on her assignments. Doesn't she Edna?" She passed the paper to Mrs. Edmonson and Gus tiptoed to see, scratching his rim of gray hair.

"If that don't beat a hen..." Gus spat contemptuously and muttered more about "riddance" and "garbage".

Shannon walked over and looked over Mrs. Edmonson's squat figure.

"It really is not Connie's writing!" Shannon declared. "Furthermore, Connie has never even dated Randy."

"That one ain't never had no date—period," Gus mused. "Probly lucky to even git one like ole Randy." He snorted disgustedly, hitching up his sagging khakis.

Monty exchanged glances with Shannon, then pulled her into the living room where no one could hear.

"Something rotten in Denmark, huh?" he asked, looking scared. "Maybe something rotten in Skull Cave? Ole Randy swore he was going back there, but I thought he was just being his usual windy self."

"I thought so too at first. But I heard them planning to sneak out and try that short cut into the cave when they got a chance. I heard him proposition her after lights out, but it wasn't to explore the cave—or to get married either. But you know how Randy is. . .his usual sleazy self."

"Knowing ole randy Randy, I can imagine," Monty agreed, shaking his head as Shannon went on.

"Connie's so vulnerable. Has she ever really had a date?"

"No, but that doesn't mean she's without experience," he said, scuffing the floor with his boot. He hesitated. "I've always heard about incest in the family. In fact, her brothers used to claim their father was into bondage and abuse with Connie. Told us at school how they'd all get lickered up and participate. Really sickening! I think everyone was relieved when those two knuckleheads dropped out of school." He paused. "I think they've got a still over near Center Point now, just a few miles from here."

"I feel so sorry for her," she said, blinking back tears. "No wonder she hid behind a wall of blubber. Who wouldn't grab the first rope, rotten or not?"

"I remember you calling it a `fort of fat'. I thought I should enlist your talent as a wordsmith to help with my lyrics. That's my weakest point." His eyes were adoring.

"Thanks," she said, loving the wonderment in his eyes, "but what can we do to help Connie? No telling what those fiends are doing to her!"

"Whatever we do could only make it worse," he suggested.

"I don't mind telling you I'm scared to break our vow of silence. Maybe it's superstition, but I half-believe Ole FOU about retribution. I don't doubt the power Satan can give his evil followers, do you?"

"Heck no, I think Satan's power is only subject to the Lords'. The Bible says so when it tells about Lucifer being cast out."

"I'm still haunted by the eyes of that guru," she confessed, shuddering. `I sensed evil there, and women's intuition tells me he's connected with this disappearance." She stopped to fight her inner battle. "We've either got to report this to the authorities or go back in that cave and check it out!" The very thought of going back to the cave affected Shannon's breathing.

"Evil can subvert men's minds; turn them into animals," he said. "But we could put our families at risk if we confront him."

Obviously taken aback at the prospect, she said slowly, "I think we have to try. . ." As those lovely green eyes challenged him, full of confidence and expectancy, he found unused reservoirs of bravado. Full of dread, he nodded.

"After all, FOU did invite us to come back through the shortcut," he declared loudly, trying to shore up his own shattered confidence. "We can do it today, pretend to explore our tunnel some more, then backtrack and take the shortcut to see if we can find any trace of Connie and Randy. Probably won't find zilch, but at least we can say we tried. O.K?"

She gulped and added, feeling her knees already beating a tatoo at the thought of such a venture."Likely, FOU's just a nut case full of illusions of grandeur. . ." Miss Cobb entered the living room at that point followed by the crowd of Seniors. Miss Cobb's voice rose shriller than usual; her freckled goiter danced as she blew her whistle and asked everyone to check their gear.

"I'm going to ask Mrs. Edmonson's husband, Delbert, to call Connie's and Randy's families to report what has happened." She added, "They are both of age, so I doubt that anything can be done. And I hope they choose to blame no one but the parties involved." She blew her whistle again. "Now, let's go finish exploring our assigned tunnels. Good hunting!"

"I could just cry—thinking about Connie," Mrs. Edmonson told Shannon as they walked toward the cave. "Poor youngun never had a real chance. She used to tell my Jenny some of the perverted things her father did. Back then, she looked like such a little blond angel, and I was afraid she had a sick mind. You know, just imagining things. Hard to believe a daddy is capable of such horror."

Shannon nodded grimly. "The man must be possessed," she said, but instead of Connie's father her mental screen flashed a picture of MostHi FOU beckoning to her.

CHAPTER XII

Miss Cobb had just used her coach's whistle and announced the imminent departure for the day of cave exploration. Seniors were converging on the cave entrance from outhouses and inside the old farmhouse when the County Sheriff and a deputy wheeled into the yard. Immediately, they dropped backpacks and lanterns to converge on his four-wheel-drive vehicle required to negotiate the precipitous mountain terrain of the area. County taxpayers had even furnished the money to install Citizens Band and other radio communications to aid in the apprehension of an increased volume of drug traffickers; the Sheriff's vehicle sported a half-dozen different kind of antennas. Dressed in stetson and khakis, the Sheriff stepped from his Jeep.

Shannon heard the squawking of the CB radio from the farmhouse bedroom where she scurried about trying to anticipate the requirements, clotheswise, of the adventure planned with Monty. As she walked out on the porch, she heard the Sheriff's loud voice reporting in on his police radio.

"Sure, this is Sheriff Bill Madden. What? Another bull butchered last night? I'll be damned! What kinda nuts are loose around here anyhow?" He laughed and repeated to his deputy,

"Ole Smitty says apparently a lotta bull nuts are loose!" He turned back to the microphone. "O.K., Smitty. I'll check 'er out. Roger an all that bull!" To the deputy, he said, "Castrated too!" He turned to Mrs. Edmonson, who stood by his Jeep listening intently.

"You heard that, I guess, Lady?" Sheriff Madden asked, removing his black stetson. "I want you and the other chaperones here to keep these young folks on a short leash. We got a rash of weird thangs goin' on hereabouts. May be connected with soma these hippie types that are trying to move drug operations back into these hills? Plantin' pot on other folks land, then booby-trapping it..."

He appeared hesitant. "Heard about local cattle left killed and castrated?"

"Not that," Mrs. Edmonson said. "Delbert did find a weirdo plowing and ran him off this farm awhile back. He even had the gall to tell Delbert he'd lived here long enough to establish squatter's rights. Course Delbert had his gun with him and told the guy he'd shoot right where the guy bent to squat if he didn't move it fast." Mrs. Edmonson's whole body shared her laughter.

Miss Cobb appeared at this point, out of breath from running.

"Did you tell the sheriff about our missing couple?" she inquired, holding her side and breathing hard. "I thought you had, Edna, but just..."

"Just getting around to it," Edna Edmonson said. She pulled the note from her apron pocket and reported the details.

"Oh Lord, wouldn't you know it would be that Randy Smith," the sheriff groaned. "He's been nothing but trouble since the army got rid of him. Well, I'll take this note and see if I can find any of his family to notify. To tell the truth, I doubt either one of them has anyone who'll be too concerned. Ole Coger's probably too drunk to care by this time of day. And if I try to notify her brothers, they may try to ambush me thinking I'm with the Revenuers. Come to think of it, maybe those two belong together. Maybe, like, take two halves and make one whole person!" He squinted at the teachers in the bright morning sunshine, laughing. He replaced his hat at a dashing angle on his dark head as he jackknifed his large body back into the seat of his vehicle. As the Jeep peeled out of the yard, he tipped his hat to the teachers and the admiring Seniors.

Monty followed Shannon inside to remind her that they must hurry to get to the cave. As he peered at her around the facing of the kitchen door, to his amazement he saw the girl slip a razor-sharp filet knife into the side of her boot. She blushed when he cleared his throat to announce his presence, then pointed at the weapon with eyes bulging while he made his adams apple dance.

"You planning to filet that sucker?" he asked, sounding incredulous.

"Having some kind of weapon makes me feel more secure," she admitted, unable to stop the slight quaver in her voice.

Raising his arms as if surrendering, he teased, "Lord help me and MostHi FOU if we anger a certain little redhead." He stopped laughing and pretended to be offended. "You don't seem to value me, macho Monty, much as a protector. Haven't you heard the *Montys* always get their man." He pulled her close in to his body, grinning down at her. To his surprise, her slender body was trembling. Responding physically, he held her.

"No, but Connie implied you always got the women," she said rallying by levity, trying to stop shaking.

"Hey, we're not going back to FOU's, not even for a tea party, if you're that scared." He laid his bronzed cheek against her hair.

"It's n-not that," she admitted, feeling a rising blush to her extreme annoyance. "We-well, if you have to know, I've just never been this close to you before. I really didn't know I had such powerful senses..."

"Do you like those sensual feelings as much as I do?" he whispered. "Maybe we should just forget this foolhardy FOU trip and come back here when the others leave. You know, make the world go away." His dark eyes had a dreamy look that did crazy things to her logical self-control.

"Remember warning Randy about Jail Bait?" she asked, hoping to restore her own perspective as well as his. He looked at her, obviously taken aback. "I didn't mean I'd ever take advantage," he said. "I was only trying to speak Randy's language so he wouldn't harass you. But face it, you do give me fever, as Elvis likes to sing." He laughed to belie the intensity in his voice.

"I know," she said, wanting to hold him in her arms. "But I don't believe in starting something I'm not ready to finish. I've learned I have strong drives, and I'm not old enough for a drivers license." She laughed, denying the force of her consuming hunger.

He said nothing, but his eyes were imploring. "Besides, we have to see about Connie. We may be her only chance to be rescued from a nightmare worse than any she has ever known. The only ones who know or care at all what happens to her."

Miss Cobb's hateful whistle-blowing restored them to sanity, and they hurried to join the others at the entrance to Skull Cave. As Monty and Shannon headed for the west tunnel, Miss Cobb called to them, asking them to wait a few minutes.

"Did you see the way those two are looking at each other?" she asked Edna Edmonson in a low voice. "I think I'd better send Gus with them."

"H-m-m, they do look luminous," Mrs. Edmonson replied. "They probably won't even have to light that lantern." Gus agreed with the teachers. So Shannon and Monty watched and exchanged disappointed groans, as Gus appointed one of the other Seniors to lead his group while he joined Monty and Shannon.

As Gus made final arrangements with his former charges, Monty whispered: "Well, you know what they say about the best laid plans of mice and men,"

"I have to admit this mouse has mixed emotions about taking that shortcut to FOU." She dropped down on a three-foot-long fallen stalactite. "On one hand, I dread going through those slimy tunnels again. But on the other hand, the possibility of encountering FOU in his torture chamber freaks me out--to the max." She watched as he lit his lantern.

"Me too, But, at least, Gus might help us if we run into trouble."

"I just wish I'd brought a couple of Mrs. Edmonson's butcher knives," she said, trying for a menacing look.

"That red hair alone turns any man into a mass of quivering jello," he teased. "But, I do wish I'd grabbed Edna's meat cleaver." Gus approached, wearing a miner's lamp on his striped railroad cap, which he always wore backwards with the bill shading his back. When Gus paused to get a "chaw" of his plug of Redman, Monty said, "I'd join him for a chaw if it'd help my nerves."

"Me too," she said, "but I'd turn so white FOU'd think I was a ghost." Their laughter relieved some of the tension.

Unwilling to reveal the secret shortcut even to Gus, the three spent most of the day traversing the narrow passage explored the first day. Finally, they crawled under the low ceilinged arch preceding the exit through the old well. The huge boulder had not been pushed back, but the door to the stairway was closed, revealing only almost invisible cracks in the limestone wall.

As they emerged into the larger tunnel, Shannon and Monty exchanged alarmed glances at the sight of a trail of blood leading back toward the chamber where they had encountered FOU. Gus was so busy investigating the ceiling and walls of the tunnel that he ignored the blood, or else, his eyesight had failed along with his hearing.

"Don't you think we should warn him there might be trouble?" Shannon asked in a low voice, sure that the nearly deaf bus driver could not hear her. As if on cue, they heard the baying of a dog from the tunnel ahead.

Suddenly they heard savage growling;a dog bounded into view,bristling. Monty grabbed her hand; then he began yelling for Gus to stop and come back. Apparently, Gus heard nothing until a huge German Shepherd rounded a column of rock and lunged at him. The dog's fangs found his throat and brought the old man to the slippery floor. Gus grabbed the dog's collar, trying to scream, but the animal seemed intent on killing his victim. Shannon ran into the melee. . . trying to pull the ferocious beast away from Gus' bloody body. Once, she kicked the dog and he turned on her for a second, then backed off barking and slobbering with rage. Before Gus could get to his feet, the guard dog landed on him once more. Realizing her one chance to save Gus, Shannon jerked the filet knife from her boot and stabbed the vicious animal in its bloody chest.

Only when it released Gus' throat, and she found the man not mortally wounded did she realize that Monty stood, white as an ice-carving on a high shelf of rock above them. His body appeared plastered against the wall and his face frozen into a mask of sheer terror. As she stared at him in total disbelief, he made an obvious effort to regain his composure. She could see his long legs shaking visibly as he climbed down from his perch.

She went over to Gus and staunched the flow of blood from his throat, as well as the bleeding gashes on his face and arms, with a first-aid kit from her backpack. Not looking at Monty, she ordered, "Help me get Gus to the stairway before we get into more trouble. We've got to get some medical help for Gus and get it quick." Gus seemed too dazed to even ask questions about the shortcut. Monty still appeared shaken, moving around as if in a trance. "What are you hung on?" she asked, letting some of her disappointment put an edge to her tone. "We must get Gus to a doctor, get him tetanus shots or whatever. O.K.?" She skirted a pool of blood. "He's losing blood fast!"

Finally, Monty responded. Walking over to where the dog's carcass lay, he picked up the bloody knife and began to sever the animal's head. "I hate to do this. Turn your head; it's pretty sickening," he ordered. "We have to take this with us and have it checked for rabies. I don't like the way this critter was slobbering and staggering. I've seen mad dogs before."

Gus looked at him in alarm. "Don't tell me I'm gonna have to take them shots in my belly," he protested. "Doggone, I'd purt near ruther die..." Afraid he might be going into shock, Shannon wrapped her sweater around his shaking body.

Monty hastened to reassure, "Oh, probably not. But having this proof might prevent it." He seemed very much the confident Monty Villines as he rose and wiped the bloody knife on his jeans. "Wait here a minute," he said. "I'm going to dash around the corner to find something to wrap this dog's head in." Holding the knife, he turned swiftly and headed for the chamber where they had encountered FOU.

Shannon's mouth formed the words of a plea for him to come back, but she knew it was useless. Every nerve and muscle in her body poised for flight or fight as the sound of his footsteps dwindled in the distance.

As she waited, Shannon's mind tried to solve the riddle of why Monty Villines would show abject fear one minute and such bravery the next. She held her breath, the better to listen for his return, aghast at his daring in bearding MostHi FOU in his den. The seconds seemed hours as she listened for any sound to indicate Monty's safety. Adrenalin spurred her heartbeat until it echoed drum-like and threatening in her own ears.

Finally, a heavy tread of boots, and she halfway expected one of the mountain men to round the tunnel with Monty slung over a massive shoulder. But, it was Monty carrying a large burlap bag. From the bag, he took another gunny sack and wrapped it around the bloody head.

She could not conceal the gladness and relief she felt at his return as she went to him and hugged him. "Did you find anything?" she asked in a low voice.

He answered in an unnaturally loud voice for Gus' benefit.

"All I found was traces of an animal carcass back there. That dog probably drug it in here. Let's get out of this place." He helped Gus to the stairway, hoping the old man, in his weakened condition, could climb the slippery steps that led to safety. When he allowed Gus to rest a moment before trying the first step over the deep well, he whispered to Shannon, "I found some other things that I'll tell you about later."

CHAPTER XIII

Shannon's concern about Gus left no time for worry about revealing FOU's secret as they half-carried the heavy driver back to the farmhouse. Monty put his jean jacket on Gus then tied the burlap bags to his back pack in order to bear most of Gus' two hundred pounds. The old man blacked out completely twice, and they stretched him out on mossy boulders while they regained their breath.

Shannon panicked at the sight of a reddish trickle in the deep wrinkles branching from the oldsters' mouth. "Oh no, he's bleeding internally. That's why he passed out!" Monty took a swipe of the liquid and sniffed. "Tobacco juice," he diagnosed. The two almost collapsed with helpless laughter and relief.

The Seniors and two teachers were milling around the Skull Cave entrance voicing their concerns about the missing parties. Then someone spotted Monty and Shannon helping Gus to the farmhouse porch. As Monty put his denim jacket under Gus' head and Shannon knelt to check his wounds, the group descended noisily on them, all bombarding them with questions at once.

"What on earth happened?" the motherly Mrs. Edmonson wailed. "We were worried sick when you were late. Afraid you were lost forever inside that man-eating mountain." She knelt with her bosoms almost touching Gus as she clucked over the deep lacerations while Monty described the dog attack.

"We were lucky to find an exit nearby from the tunnel," Monty explained. "The old tunnel must make a tremendous loop that ends up almost back at the mouth of the cave."

"I wouldn't say you were just lucky, son," Mrs. Edmonson said with tears brimming in her eyes. Her voice became husky. "I've lived right here by this cave all these years and never suspected there was an exit on our farm. I'd say the Lord took your hand an led you outa there." She checked Gus' pulse and became flustered. "This man would've never made it coming back the long way. We gotta git some medical help, quick." She bent to examine Gus. "He just lost consciousness! Probably done lost too much blood."

"Want me to drive him into the clinic near Jasper?" Monty asked, looking grim. As Shannon ran to get her wallet, planning to accompany him, he said to Miss Cobb, "I may have solved the mystery of cattle being killed and castrated around here. It looked like that dog had dragged parts of one through the cave tunnel. You might call the sheriff and tell him I killed the dog and am taking its head in to be tested for rabies." *I killed the dog?? He felt such shame. I can't believe I said I killed it. Why can't I face the truth?*

Two other Senior boys helped Monty make a bed for Gus on the back seat of the old school bus and carry him aboard. Then Shannon returned and sat down beside Gus, holding his grease stained hand as they careened around the winding steep curves of the mountain road.

"What in hell is this?" Bill Garton, Monty's friend asked, kicking the bloody burlap bag Monty had stowed under the front seat.

Monty glanced away from the road back toward where Gus lay. He used delaying tactics to stop the questions about Gus' injury, as he inquired, "He can't hear can he? I don't want to alarm him."

"You kiddin?" Bill said. Kevin, the other Senior, shook his head. "He can't hear himself fart when there's nothing whatever wrong with him." The other Senior nodded, laughing.

"Well, I guess you're right. Anyway, thats the head of the dog that attacked Gus. The way it was staggering and slobbering, I think it was mad. But I want to be certain before poor ole Gus has to take those awful shots for rabies. He said he'd rather be dead."

"The way his pulse is acting, we may not have to worry about rabies shots," Shannon said, looking at them with eyes shimmering with tears, as she plied Miss Cobb's stethoscope again.

The other Seniors seemed to finally realize the gravity of Gus' condition. "We'll help carry him in," they offered hovering Monty as he pushed the old bus to its limit, looking tense and drained. Bill sobered until he looked almost old enough for the handlebar mustache he was trying to grow.

As soon as the Emergency Room doctor began treating Gus, Monty asked Shannon and the Seniors to remain with the injured man.

"I want to take that dog's head for analysis," he explained, "so the doctor will know as soon as possible whether to start shots." He started out.

"By all means," the young doctor agreed, looking up from swabbing Gus' wounds. "With head wounds, this is urgent, since the rabies affects the brain sooner in head wounds." Whole blood coursed into Gus' unconscious body.

Later, Monty pulled the old bus across the Buffalo River bridge on the curve leading into the picturesque mountain hamlet. His eyes stayed immune to the riot of flowers around the ancient courthouse square. He parked the bus behind the courthouse by a graceful gazebo and sat there with his head in his hands. Connie's tortured face as it had been at thirteen in Red Star swam like a video before his eyes. He could still hear her broken cry, "Please don't, Daddy!" as her drunken father pushed the child rudely from behind the steering wheel and climbed in beside her. And Connie's child-like eyes still followed him, accusatory and begging: "Somebody help me; if there's anybody out there that thinks I'm worth saving, do something!" *She's like the child from an orphan's home who left a crudely printed note reading: "Whoever finds this note - I love you." he thought sadly.*

But the next video that played the screen of his tortured mind hurt even more: Seeing himself roosting like some big chicken while Shannon saved Gus. Then watching himself crash from his pedestel in those lovely green eyes. He moaned once more, then got up dejectedly and carried the bloody burlap bag into the County Coroner's office, dogged by the conviction: *If Gus dies, it will be my fault; I should've warned him, or at least intervened to save him from that maddog.*

CHAPTER XIV

When Monty and Shannon returned with the school bus and discouraging news about Gus' condition, the teachers had the exploring party all packed to return to Kingsville. "I wanted to fix breakfast," said Mrs. Edmonson,"but nobody could eat."

"Sheriff Madden suggested further exploration of the cave might be pressing our luck," Miss Cobb told Monty and Shannon, looking relieved. "Seems another mutilated animal was found last night. Freshy killed, so they know that dog' didn't do it. He says people are claiming it's everything from aliens to Satanic cults that's behind it."

Monty and Shannon exchanged knowing looks. Monty fought an inner battle, shuffling nervously, then muttering, "I'm ready to head home. I've never been so beat in my life."

"I'm really sorry this happened," Mrs. Edmonson said, hugging Shannon. "You both look so tired and depressed. I'll keep Gus and you two in my prayers and let you know how ole Gus gets along. I'm hoping his heart condition will improve and he won't have to take those rabies shots."

Everyone thanked Mrs. Edmonson for her hospitality, including Miss Cobb, before she herded the last stragglers aboard the old bus. Monty drove, checking Bill out on handling the cranky crate as they followed the narrow spirals of road out of the Buffalo River Valley. "I guess I could drive on to Kingsville if you're afraid of chauffeuring," Monty offered. But Bill Garton confidently told Monty, "Man, I can drive anything that runs. And, I know I'd be safer than you. You look dead on your feet."

As Shannon watched Monty at the wheel, she agreed with Bill's assessment. In fact, the whole crowd seemed somber and sad, and she felt the same. *Monty really had not acted or looked like himself since the dog's attack.* Although she still could not fathom why he had failed to come to Gus' aid or hers during the attack, she pushed the thought of that away and concentrated on his later behavior. Now, she felt his pain in a way she had never experienced before.

When he surrendered the wheel to Bill at the entrance to his father's Flying V horse ranch and came to sit beside her, she searched for words to alleviate his obvious depression.

"I hope you're not blaming yourself for what happened," she said in a low voice, putting her chin on his shoulder in spite of Miss Cobb's constant scrutiny. "Life's not fair. But I think there's a master plan for our lives. That even the bad things later benefit us if we listen to the Master." I wish I could cradle him and kiss where it hurts, she thought, yearning to comfort him.

"I know," he agreed, without conviction. "Just makes me sick I can't go back and change a coupla bad decisions."

"Who hasn't wished that?" she asked sympathetically squeezing his muscular arm. He studied her face as if to imprint it in his memory.

Although Shannon had visited the Flying V once as a child, she had forgotten the loveliness of the long valley in which it lay. Monty's home, a ranch-style log house, nestled into a hillside overlooking two thousand acres of meadows that followed the scallops of the sparkling Buffalo River. Herds of Arabians raised beautifully shaped heads to watch the old bus follow the curving descent to the valley floor. A mare shied at the noise. She raced with mane and tail flowing in the breeze, followed by her frolicking colt, toward the soaring white cliffs bordering the river.

"If my Great Granddad had to sell this," she said wistfully, "I'm glad he was smart enough to sell it to your family."

"I think it would kill my dad to lose it," he said, looking out across the green spread that ran as far as the eye could see. "You know Thomas Hart Benton used to come down here every summer to paint. He stayed with us, and I used to want to be just like him. I even tried my hand at painting with Mr. Benton. Got so frustrated I almost cut an ear off like that French artist. He said that our valley reminded him of that movie made in Wales called *How Green Was My Valley.*"

"It does me too!" she exclaimed. "I've watched that about three times on the late show, and I love it. As a kid, I pretended to be Annharad."

"I can't really imagine ever living anywhere else," he admitted. "But the way things are going with my dad and the agricultural economy, I may have to learn to." He looked at her with despair in his dark eyes. Then he squeezed her hand and said, "Goodbye". Not "I'll be seeing you soon, I hope." Not anything that her heart yearned to hear from his lips. Just "Goodbye" as he walked to the front of the bus before Bill even brought it to a stop. *As if he's in a hurry to leave this-group and the memory that goes with it behind.* Shannon blinked back the tears at the thought she had never been more than a passing interest. *No incandescence in my presence?*

Bill brought the vehicle to a clattering stop in front of the ranchhouse porch. Gray-haired Mattie Villines watched her son approach with a vein-corded hand shading her eyes from the sun-glint of the Buffalo and Steel Creek whirlpool created by their intersection nearby. Shannon observed that the lot of the large show-barn held several horses, whinneying a welcome to Monty while their colts frisked nearby.

Shannon leaned out the window, waving as Monty stood watching the bus. If only I could hold him close, kiss away the quotation marks of pain between those sad eyes, she thought, watching him diminish in size as the bus pulled away. Missy Evans dropped into the seat beside Shannon.

Shannon averted her face, staring out over the Flying V with misty eyes as the bus climbed the mountain, pretending to be unaware of Missy's triumphant glances. I can't let her gloat over my tears, vowed Shannon.

"Well, looks like superstud Monty made another conquest," Missy jeered. "Thank God and Greyhound he's gone. And I don't have to stay on this hick-trip any longer." Shannon ignored the blonde until she rose and flounced away.

As she joined some of the other girls in the back of the bus, Shannon heard her say, "At least, this trip accomplished one thing. Got rid of that Pain-in-the-Butt Connie. Maybe she found somebody to sleep with beside her brothers."

Shannon fought back more tears as Missy continued, talking in a very loud voice and watching Shannon: "Guess what, Shannon got her learner's permit on this trip. Oh, not to drive! She's too young for that." Shannon tried not to wince visibly as they all laughed.

CHAPTER XV

As the yellow school bus disappeared in a cloud of dust on the graveled road, Monty watched it go, feeling as if his life had just pulled away with Shannon. Overwhelmed with a sense of loss, he stood there after the dust had drifted over the pastures and dispersed. *It's almost like the first time my mother left me alone at five in the hospital, three days after the dog attacked. When she got sick, I felt like part of me had been ripped away, that I'd be too crippled to ever go on alone. I know Dad thought I was a wimp to be afraid of dogs; he told me so often enough, even there at the hospital when I kept having nightmares. What must Shannon think? A grown man acting like a scared child, allowing a fragile girl to save ole Gus.* His upper cheeks burned all the way to his lower cheeks every time he ran a mental image of himself plastered against the wall on that shelf of rock in the cave. *How could I have become so obsessed with Shannon in such a short time? Then, to fail her so miserably.* He felt like a man tied with rawhide to stakes in a den of fireants when he recalled the disbelief in her eyes.

Stop it, he told himself, turning to answer his mother's shrill summons from the porch. She still watched him, her brow furrowed with anxiety, as he approached. "What's wrong, son? Why are you dragging your tail?" she asked. "How come you're home early?" Dentureless, she shielded her mouth.

"Aw, nothing to worry about, Mom," he assured her, feeling inadequate to talk about Connie or Gus at the moment. "Everyone just got tired,"

"Who's that pretty redhead that waved at you?" she asked, studying his reaction closely. She lisped with a toothless grin, "Lost them fool teeth again."

"Um, that's Shannon Ceranda. You know, she was in the Senior Play. Jim Ceranda's daughter from over in the Kings River Valley. Steel Creek was named for her Great Grandpa Steel."

Just then, his father approached from the stables, leading their new Arabian stallion. "What happened, son?" he asked. Dallas Villines had the same striking darkness of the Black Villines men as his son. His face and body still retained a tanned, rugged look from long hours of outdoor work. But Monty realized as he looked anew at his father that the sideburns had turned white in the past few months. Genetic facial creases had deepened. Dad's looking old and beaten, he thought with deepening depression.

"Well, for one thing, Connie Coger eloped with ole Randy Smith," he admitted, figuring his father might have heard it if he'd been into Boxley. "Course, the teachers got all upset, thinking the parents might blame them. So they cut the cave exploration short."

"Yow, I heard that this mornin." Then his father asked curiously, "What was it like inside there? Soma my buddies tried to get up a treasure-hunting trip onct. But it fizzled out. Find anything?"

"Only a pretty redhead from what I observed as the bus left," his mother teased. "Let Monty get cleaned up and ready to eat. He looks pooped."

"You got an answer from your application at the University of Arkansas," his father said, clapping him on the shoulder as they went inside. "Think you'll settle on that one?"

Monty surprised himself with a sudden revelation, turning to his father. "You know, dad. I've decided I don't want to go to college—not now anyhow. Later, I may try Nashville. But, even before that, I'm thinking I might take Uncle Frank up on that insurance job he offered me, at least for the summer. That way, I could maybe help some around here. Even make me a grub-stake for Nashville."

His father's face showed relief for a moment, then his direct gaze turned questioning. "You're not backing off on college just because you know I'm short of cash are you, son? We'd get a loan or something if you want to go. You know that, don't you? I'd about sell pencils on a street corner to give you an opportunity I never had."

His mother eyed her men affectionately.

"He probably just don't want to leave that little redhead," she teased. "I seen the fond way she looked at him as she waved goodbye. She looks like a keeper to me! You recollect the pretty one in the play, Dal? One in green with them green eyes, Jim Ceranda's girl."

"The one stacked like a brick outhouse?" Dal asked, "Who'd fergit her?" He jiggled his eyebrows at Monty, grinning.

"Well," Mattie drawled, I don't think no outhouse ever moved our son like thatun." She rumpled his tousled black hair.

"Naw, Mom. I really just don't wanta leave your cookin,'" Monty teased, hugging her dumpy figure. "But I am going to see Uncle Frank after I get some chow and some rest."

"Your dad teased me while you were gone," she confided as they headed kitchenward, following the delightful aroma of breakfast. "You know how I'm always taking my false teeth out and putting them in my apron pocket?" He nodded, twinkling down at her, taking comfort in her adoring eyes, the way she laughed—making her chins shake. *Like a chubby, toothless child.*

"Well, I lost them teeth when I went to see about Ole Bounty's new foal down by the river yesterday," she went on, laughing until she could hardly talk. "So your daddy says, 'What you need do, Mattie, is tie one of your big biscuits on a strang an run back the way you went yesterday. Them dentures'll grab it for shore!'" Their laughter blended into a symphony of home.

Monty poured himself a cup of coffee, beginning to feel a spark of hope. Just making a decision about his future had lifted his mood.

"Know what she said, son?" Dallas Villines chuckled, dropping into his chair at the head of the table. He looked fondly at Mattie as she served the hearty breakfast of home-cured ham, sawmill gravy and big biscuits. Holding one of the fluffy biscuits aloft, he yodeled, "Take yore own choppers, Dal; they grab 'em twict as fast as mine!'

As Monty laughed, his appetite returned full-force. Now, I'll have a chance to redeem myself with Shannon, his heart sang, as he heaped his plate with food.

CHAPTER XVI

True to his impulsive offer to try the insurance business, when Monty encountered his Uncle Frank Villines at the Boxley store the next morning, he informed Frank of his decision. Uncle Frank had been a widower for five years until recently when he married Opal Findley, an ardent Pentecostal from Compton with a fetish of absolute sanitation. After expressing delight that his nephew had finally embraced the career Frank had long envisioned for Monty, Frank joined the group around the pot-bellied stove. Although the May Monday felt balmy; sitting around the stove always seemed to promote conviviality, tethering this generation to all the previous ones that had gathered here. The store had been passed down through the Villines family almost since the first Villines pulled across the Buffalo River with his family in a tall-wheeled covered wagon.

Uncle Frank crooked a finger at Monty, who was fishing a soft drink out of the Coke machine, and announced Monty's decision to his cronies. Monty pushed his Stetson back, grinning.

"Any of you men need insurance on everything from your bidies to your pickups, here's your man," Uncle Frank announced proudly with an arm around Monty's shoulders. "We gotta help him make enough money to try his luck in Nashville, boys! Thisun can write you a song an then sing it the best you ever heard. Beats ole George Jones by a country mile an don't get drunk an miss shows!"

"Well, it takes a very unique talent to make it in Nashville," Monty said. "Also it takes enough money to hang on there and wait for the breaks." Frank boxed his nephew affectionately.

"An that's the reason I'm settin you up with an appointment with our not-too-distant cousin, Kirby," Frank yodeled. "Here, pretend you wanta sell ole Charlie here some life insurance," he ordered, coaching Monty as Charlie offered unyielding resistance to every suggestion Monty could think of on the spur of the moment. Monty even surprised himself with his ability to side-step Charlie's resistence to his sales spiel.

"Why, you're a born insurance salesman, son!" Uncle Frank announced. "I'm just going to turn my appointment with ole Kirby over to you. Can you drive out to his farm in about an hour? I want you to strike while your iron is hot! You can't miss on ole Kirby. Just remind him you're cousins. If he don't want no insurance on his or Irene's bidies, then ask about his pickup and farm machinery."

"Well, O.K.," Monty agreed, feeling a bit more confident. "Where's the forms? What do I need besides an application?"

"Well, I got my office in my back bedroom. But, tell you what, you just dash by my house and I'll have Opal give you the packet of forms. You ain't met my bride, Opal, yet have you?" Pulling on his red suspenders, he inflated what remained of a chest above his belt bukle, cinched above a pot-belly, then rose on his toes like a tall rooster preparing to crow. "They named her Opal because they recognized a jewel right off!" he said, looking over his hornrims and grinning at Monty. "Opal was moppin' when she shooed me out this mornin' and told me not to come back until she had time to wax, and then to come in barefooted. I swear that woman mops ever day exceptin' Sunday, which she spends talking in tongues at that church of hern."

The other cronies of Frank were all nodding and winking at Monty.

"Opal even mops my office, maybe even to our yard—but she oughta be done by the time you get there. That's the only fault I find with my bride. She's so durned tidy she can't hardly find time for no other wifely duties." His hoary eyebrows did a suggestive dance as he asked, "Know what I mean? In fact, she tries to make me boil it 'fore I use it." He nudged Monty in the ribs, cackling with ribald laughter along with the other senior citizens in the group.

"Well, with a seventy-year-old, that ain't but about onct a year, is it Frank?" asked Charlie Villines, co-owner of the country store, winking at the others. "I hear she makes you go huntin' in the rain and stay all day so you won't track up her floors."

"That's a dirty lie!" yelled Frank, directing a baleful look at his cronies from two heavy eyebrows that had merged into one. "She makes me go so I won't sneak up on her while she's bent over!"

Before they all stopped chuckling, Monty asked, "You still got those Walker hounds, Uncle Frank?" He watched Uncle DeVoe whittle into the spittoon, thinking of all the memories this little store conjured up: his dad shaking out his last nickel for a Big Chief school tablet, his mother deciding what to buy while waiting to sell a basket of eggs fresh from the Domineckers. "I ran by to meet your new bride one evening, and them boogers raised such a rukus, I didn't even get outa my pickup." Frank had to wait to finish a domino move before he could answer Monty.

"Yow, I still got 'em. But I keep 'em penned since they brought down a bear over in Booger Holler other day. I mean they about et that bear, hide an' all 'fore I could git 'em to turn loose. Killed that ole booger dead as a doornail."

"Uh-oh, guys, here comes that pritty Gibbins gal from up by Jasper," Charlie cautioned. "Clean up your act. You, Monty, set that Stetson at a cool angle." Uncle Frank clowned and primped by placing his few remaining strands of black hair carefully across his bald head.

"Really considerate not dazzling her with the shine from that head, Uncle Frank," Monty teased. "Well, tell Aunt Opal I'll see her shortly." He looked down at his jeans and boots. "Do I need to put on a suit and tie? You know, try to look professional?" The Gibbins girl entered and did a visible double-take at Monty, who tipped his hat to her.

"I hardly think so, son," Uncle Frank whispered. "You just passed the test. I know now you can sell Kirby's wife even if she ain't related like ole Kirby is." He walked to the telephone on the wall and cranked the handle on one side to summon the operator. "I'm calling Opal now," he said as he waited for the operator. "Howdy, Pearlie May," Monty heard him greet the switchboard operator, visiting a moment before she rang Opal. After listening a few minutes to his wife, he gave Monty a signal that everything was "GO" with a forefinger circled to his thumb as he gave Opal instructions about which insurance forms to collect for Monty.

Monty left the store hurriedly when Charlie yelled, "Frank ast Opal if she heard anything on the party line about that Kingsville bus driver gettin' attacked by a maddog." Then Uncle Frank yelled back, and Charlie shouted, "You mean Monty didn't tell you nothing about killing it? Way the womenfolk are tellin' it, Monty was quite a hero." Monty kept his back to the men lest they see the crimson tide of shame crest in his face.

As Monty drove, he decided to go ahead and pick up the forms in order to study them before keeping his appointment with Kirby. His mind became so tormented with guilt that he found himself driving as if pursued by the devil. *Now, I told one little lie, and they're trying to turn me into a hero. Oh -God, maybe I shouldn't even try to wrap this pickup around this curve, just let it fly off into that vast abyss below this mountain top. What if Shannon learns I claimed to have killed that dog? She likely already thinks I'm a coward. Now she knows I'm a liar. But I'll never have a chance to change her impression if I don't make it on this insurance job, because it's my only chance to stay around here. But what do I know about selling insurance? I'll probably make a damn fool of myself there too. If I fail at this, I may go to Nashville and be too embarrassed to ever see any of them again after I fail there too.* To stop his plunge into despair, he decided: I'll remember Shanny's face as the bus pulled away. And dad's when I told him I'd stay and help.

Recalling what Shannon had said about a Master plan, he slowed down as he approached Frank's rural home and found himself making an unspoken mental supplication. He pulled up in front of Frank's mail box and saw a rotund little woman emerge from the farmhouse carrying a packet of forms. With vast relief, Monty noticed the absence of the hunting dogs, although he could hear their baying from somewhere in the back of the house. He suppressed a grin at Aunt Opal's resemblance to a horned owl with two huge rolls of gray hair at each side of her forehead, dark horn-rims over solemn large eyes and a tiny hooked nose. His memory kept re-running Uncle Frank's comments about his bride, creating such comedic pictures that Monty could scarcely contain his humor. Part of Aunt Opal's hair had been rolled around Sunkist orange juice cans, but a gray-striped torrent of it still flowed down her plump shoulders. She wore a print housecoat and Mother Comforts that revealed a vast network of varicose veins, and she did not appear exhilirated to see Monty.

When he introduced himself as her nephew, she almost smiled but the tight pucker held. "I brung the insurance forms outside," she said primly, wiping the beads of sweat back toward her big pompadours. "I just waxed and it ain't dry." Just as she handed Monty the forms, he felt his neck hairs bristle as howls and scurrying feet interrupted their pleasantries. To his horror, three monstrous hell-hounds came barreling around the farm-house on two legs, slavering over bared teeth, growling savagely. All three lunged for his throat! One got his collar, another his shirt, popping buttons. The third grabbed his ankle, after leaving muddy paw marks down his front and back, unzipping his fly with a toenail.

Above their crazed yammering, Aunt Opal shrieked shrilly and ineffectively, "Down Samson! Stop it, Goliath! Git, Abe!" She kicked, throwing a shoe.

Instinctively, Monty grabbed Aunt Opal and thrust her toward the crazed creatures, thinking they would not bite their mistress (if he was capable of thinking at all at this point.) The dogs' ferocity left no doubt that they intended to kill him just as they had that black bear. Using his poor auntie like a training dummy, he shook her at each lunging brute, blocking its charge, while Aunt Opal's curlers clattered down on the rocky driveway. He saw one of the hounds gobble Aunt Opal's glasses as they fell, before her shrill petitions to the Almighty finally returned a remnant of sanity to his fear-addled brain.

As dog fangs crunched his other ankle and Aunt Opal tried vainly to dislodge Goliath from his fly, he kicked the slobbering fiend in its bared teeth with the other foot, almost bringing all of them to the ground. Then, Aunt Opal's blood-clabbering yell chilled his brain back from a numb lump into a reasoning apparatus.

"Oh, God help, he bit me!" she squalled, grabbing her rear.

Somehow, he got his shaking legs in gear enough to kick the other attacking dogs hard enough to send them yelping.

With her bulging, terror-stricken eyes, Aunt Opal resembled an overstuffed, bedraggled Cabbage Patch doll that had been the plaything of ruffians. Her streaming hair lay plastered to her tear-dribbled cheeks and sweaty back. But, Monty was still so out of control that he asked his prim, super-religious little auntie to show him where she had been bitten. Later, he could not believe he had actually asked this and even attempted to touch the spot by fondling her plump hip and asking, "Here, Aunt Opal?"

Her shocked outrage finally registered in his lame brain, and he jerked his hand away as if her hip had already developed a raging fever. Blood began beading down her leg, and he found himself asking stupidly,

"Can I help treating that wound?"

She glared at him, speechless with rage.

"I meant I'd take you to the doctor," he blurted, already imagining her telling this story over the party line.

"No!" she retorted stiffly, limping toward the house. Holding her hip, she yelled back over her shoulder, "You've done too much already, Buster! Hope none of my neighbors was passin' an starts a story about my virtue."

CHAPTER XVII

As the Seniors filed into the Kingsville Baptist Church for the Baccalaureate, Monty glimpsed Shannon. Pulse racing, he tossed the red tassel of his mortarboard away from his eyes, hoping he didn't look as stupid as he felt in the inverted-crock-pot-cap. Then his glance caught his family seated behind the Seniors, and he felt himself redden and grow sweaty under the heavy graduation gown.

Grandma Villines was whipping out a paper bag from her huge battered purse. She peeled back the stiff sack with a loud crackle and tilted the quart jar to drink. His parents looked embarrassed as a battery of eyes zeroed in on the oblivious, starchy old lady. Monty dropped into the pew beside Bill Garton, groaning, "Oh, no. Grandma brought that infernal mineral water in a poke. Now, these Baptists probably think it's moonshine!" Bill's snort and the smirks on every side added to Monty's chagrin.

He registered little of the sermon due to his inner accusers: *"You've really ripped your britches with Shannon now. She knew you were a coward. Now the whole community is laughing over your using your aunt as an attack dummy.* Torn between his desire to talk to Shannon and his fear of her contempt, he rose when the sermon ended and followed his classmates toward the exit, head lowered, afraid to see if the girl had already left.

But a lilting voice stopped him near an alcove by the entrance. He found himself looking down into clear green eyes. Her coppery curls, upswept at the sides, emphasizd her tilted nose and the delicately shaded eyes, the long lashes that tangled where they met. Shannon looked solemn.

"Heard anything from Gus?" she asked. Before he could answer, she added, "Or about Connie and what happened to those two? They're telling awful tales. Just wish I knew she was O.K." Her eyes filled with tears. " I keep having nightmares of her with that devil, don't you?"

"Oh, God, yes," he whispered passionately. "Just wish I knew what to do—whether it might help or make things worse."

"Yow, me too. I keep thinking we should've called the sheriff."

He swallowed several times, in obvious pain when he realizd

she did not yet know the worst. He shuffled his feet, dreading to tell her. *I'll probably cry if she does.*

"Me too, " he admitted. "I keep thinking Gus would be alive if. . ."

"What? You mean Gus died?" she asked, looking stunned. Pulling her into the nearby alcove, he held her close for a blissful moment as she stifled her sobs. The crowd that had been shuffling by them seemed to disappear leaving the two in a time warp.

"Yow, last night. His heart. Happened before the rabies test even got back. But it was positive." He studied her slender hands and arms anxiously. "You didn't have any scratches or claw marks, did you?" She shook her head, and he breathed again. "Thank God! Thought about that all night last night!" As he held her fragile figure, he knew the primal protectiveness of the first cave man with his woman. He wiped a tear from her cheek with a big finger, knowing that his destiny had just come into focus. All the first times of his dreams combined in the feel of her curves against him. He tilted her heart-shaped face, tracing its lovely petal softness with his forefingers, imprinting its dewey freshness in his senses. Just as he bent to kiss her, reality brought the two thudding to earth.

"Shanny," her father shouted, barreling toward them with the ominous look of a tornado as the crowd stopped to stare.

"Uh-oh," Monty gulped. He turned his back on danger. "I've got to talk to you before I leave for Nashville!" Desperately head-motioning back toward her father, he asked, "Any chance he would let me take you out?"

"Um, not likely," she said, reading the approaching storm warnings. "Dad won't even let me car date yet. "She gave him one of those direct looks that seemed to see into his soul. "Nashville?" she blurted. "I thought you were going to college!"

"Well, my dad's ranch is in trouble, so I decided to launch out and see if I can make it in the music business. About as much chance as a snowball in July, as they say. I'll probably starve out and come home like a whipped hound." He gave her another of those farewell looks.

She studied him through several layers of tears. "You kiddin? With your talent, you'll make it for sure." And I'll lose you for sure, her heart reported. *Why does he look so depressed, not at all excited at the propect of tackling Nashville, finding a showcase for his talent?*

"I wish we could talk, but I'm leaving tomorrow," he said. "I understand why you won't go out with me though." He turned and left swiftly, holding his motarboard under one arm as he joined the other Seniors.

She didn't even ask her father to go out with me, he thought; she's so disappointed in me that she was just making an excuse. I'm glad I'm shaking the dust of this place off my boots, he decided as he strode toward his old pickup and angrily shucked off the red gown, tossing it into the pickup with the red mortarboard cap. He clamped his Stetson down, then turned on the ignition, and peeled away.

She probably heard the whole town laughing about my latest goof-up at Uncle Frank's. That Opal wouldn't let her dresstail touch her until she told the story to anyone that would listen. He could imagine Frank and his cronies rolling on the floor with laughter about it at the Boxley store. People seemed so bored with small-town life that they spiced it up by making gossip more sensational, comedy twice as funny. But worse than Shannon's laughter would be her pity. And that's what I saw in those green eyes, he decided, gunning his roaring steed to its limit.

CHAPTER XVIII

For a few days after the Senior Trip, Shannon wandered around in a happy daze, eliciting much teasing from Tod, her younger brother. Scolding from her mother followed when the girl parked the meat in the pantry rather than the refrigerator while doing her kitchen chores. Her absent-minded mistake only became apparent when Josie Ceranda followed her nose to the source of the awful stench.

"I just don't know what's gotten into that girl," she complained to her husband, watching Shannon move away like a starry-eyed sleep-walker, as she ironed Keith's college laundry.

"The love bug bit her," Tod declared, trying to look wise beyond his thirteen years. "She's been bird-doggin' that mail box every day."

"Aw, just another stage in the evolution of a woman," surmised Jim Ceranda.

"And you've taught Dad all the stages a woman goes through, huh, Ma?" wise-cracked Tim, the brother just older than Shannon. Tim, at the age to appear all feet and ears, peered into the refrigerator in a worshipful way while gobbling a chicken leg.

"Matter of fact, I have to take credit for that," boasted Keith, the blond giant of the family, now a Nose Guard on the Razorback team at the University of Arkansas at Fayetteville. "Especially about the cave-woman-stage where I had to start." Tim nodded emphatically and gave Tod a high-five.

"I've been hearing some mighty strange rumors about that cave trip," Jim said. "About a dozen different stories about how Gus got attacked by that maddog. Then all those awful things people are saying about Connie Coger."

"Yow, some really juicy gossip about Connie and Randy," Keith agreed. "Did Shannon say much about that?" He looked from one parent to the other.

Tim answered for his parents, still looking in the fridge. His speech required an interpreter of the full-mouth syndrome. As his mother frowned, he swallowed mightily and said "She got mad when I asked." He turned to his mother. "She say anything to you?" His mother shook her head and shrugged.

"Just how sorry she feels for Connie. That the girl seemed so vulnerable." his mother said. Noting Tod's avid curiosity, she ordered, "Toddy, would you run down and turn the baby calves in with their mothers?" He went through the door very slowly and lingered within earshot as his older brother went on.

"You know they're telling Connie is pregnant by her father or her brothers. Not to mention Randy. I know you can't believe gossip, but some of the things those hillbilly brothers of hers used to tell us guys at school. Well, nothing would surprise me."

"But, if the girl is pregnant, why jump from the frying pan to ole Randy's fire?" Jim Ceranda asked. "Everyone around knows ole Randy's worthless as tits on a boar-hog. Been from one escapade to another ever since Viet Nam."

"Uh-oh, here comes Shannon," her mother warned. "She says all this about Connie is small-town gossip and shouldn't be repeated. It upset her when I brought it up, so let's be talking about the weather." She began humming, keeping time with her steam iron as the girl drifted into the room, followed closely by Tod. "What did the weather report predict for tomorrow?" she asked.

"Hey, Shanny," Tod began. "Did you notice how hot that auditorium was at Graduation? Or how everyone kept gawking toward the door every time somebody came in, thinking it might be Connie Coger or Randy Smith?" His parents both gave him the bad eye, but the adolescent refused to recognize the warning looks. "Um, sis, you said Monty Villines caught my bats. He's mucho macho, ain't he, Sis?" He pinched a disgusting hicky-horn on his forehead, wincing.

"Sure, he's neat," she agreed, backing away, escaping to her room with more haste than she had shown since the cave exploration.

Once there, she fell across her purple canopied bed and looked pensively out over the broad expanse of meadows that bordered the Kings River, retreating once more into a re-run of her last encounter with Monty.

CHAPTER XIX

The rural mail carrier had barely braked to a stop at the Ceranda's mailbox when Shannon went racing down the steep hill from her home. Her mother, father and Keith stood on the second story balcony behind the white columns watching the girl.

"Toddy's right," her mother said, "she has been birddogging the mail box. Probably can't give up hoping she'll hear from that Villines boy she met on the Senior Trip." She donned a sappy expression and waltzed around her husband. "Aw to be sixteen again, in love, and waiting for my first letter from you, Prince Charmin!"

"Well, you had reason enough to be in a trance," he acknowledged, preening like an Adonis to make his son laugh. "But, Shanny---she's a different matter. She just hasn't seemed like herself since that Senior cave trip. Has she even talked much about it to you, Josie?" His wife and son both shook their heads.

"Now, you know that just ain't Shanny. She's usually so wound up with the excitement of even the most ordinary trip. You notice how preoccupied she is; why she don't even fight with Toddy when he torments her."

"Right," Keith agreed thoughtfully. "But she did get upset the other night when she dozed off in front of the fire on the divan. You know how she was muttering and thrashing around, saying something about Skull Cave?"

"You know, I asked her what the inside of that place was like, and she just said, 'About what you'd expect. . . .' Ain't like her to clam up like that. Know what I mean?" Jim Ceranda looked worried." Or to look sad. That little face purt near makes me bawl."

"Well, Toddy's teasing didn't help," Josephine Ceranda added, laughing. "Remember how that little scamp made up a story about what she'd said in her sleep? Puttin' on that goofy cow-owed look, leaning back on Tim's chest and moaning, 'Oh, Monty, you're such a hunk! Can I lay my head on your manly chest?" Her Irish face flushed and her green eyes danced with merriment.

Kieth looked unusually serious as he turned to his father. "Shanny told me Monty had left for Nashville and she wished she hadn't turned him down for a date—even if she had to defy your dating rules, dad."

Jim Ceranda, straightened like a stallion that had been reined to a sudden halt. "Well," he assured Keith, "maybe the Lord escorted that young man away awhile to let my Shanny grow up! You sound a bit critical, like I'm over-protective, son. But that girl was sick so long, that I'm afraid she's not as advanced on dating and such as some sixteen-year-olds."

"She's as mature as a lot of the college girls I date, dad," Keith said. "Even more so than most, and not half as manipulative. I think that long bout with Mono gave her perspective on adolescence." He hooked his big thumbs in his overall bib. "Course, my advice on controlling her glands instead of them rulin' her didn't hurt."

"I ain't raised no fools yet, son," Jim said fondly, clapping Keith on his bulging bicep. He leaned forward, still watching Shannon's long jean-clad legs fly down the winding road from their hilltop home. "Too bad you didn't profit from a spell of Mono 'fore I had to rescue you from yore folly with that boy-crazy Allen gal!"

"How you think I got so wise?" Keith asked, grinning. "Poor kid," Keith said. "I hate to see that sad face if she never got a letter again. I tried to warn her yesterday about expecting too much from an older guy like ole Monty. Told her his dad reported Monty had already gotten an audition through some guy he met at OSU who's a record producer in Nashville. Maybe, I shouldn't have, but I told her there's always dozens of groupies hanging around the studios eager to do anything just to get one of those guys to speak to them."

"With all that comfort, I'm surprised she didn't kill herself, Keith," his mother said, watching the mailman stuff a bunch of letters in the box and pull away.

"Lookit that little tomboy go!" her father boasted pridefully, still watching Shannon as she neared the mailbox. "Why, she's kickin' sparks outa them flint rocks; better time than she done at the track meet last year."

"Uh-oh," Keith yelled, "Enemy fighter at nine o'clock! Ole Tod's going to beat her to the mailbox for sure. I don't think she's even seen him yet!" Sure enough, Tod had raced from the barn where he had been feeding calves, and he grabbed the letters just as Shannon neared her goal. Sorting hastily, he held a letter aloft, and his family heard his jubilant taunting as the girl panted up to him and began jumping and clawing at the letter. They could also hear her infuriated screeching as she chased the agile thirteen-year-old, But his height enabled him to hold the letter tantalizingly aloft even when she tore his chambray shirt off and laid skid marks down his pimpled back with her long nails.

Running for his pickup, Jim called back, "I'd best get down there 'fore she scobs his knob for him!" He gunned away, throwing sludge from the fresh cow patties in the pasture in front of the house.

In a few minutes, he returned with Shannon, who remained in the pickup as he brought the rest of the mail inside.

"She got it!" he chuckled. "I could barely tear her away from reading the Villines boy's letter long enough to get her into the pickup." They all stood watching the girl as she sat with eyes glued to the shaking stationery in her hands.

"You seem to be tolerating this romance a lot better, Jim, now that the young man is about two hundred miles south," Josie Ceranda teased, patting her husband's buns as he bent over the wrought iron railing, his eyes intent on his daughter's expressive face. "I can almost read his letter by watching her darlin' face," Josie said, misty-eyed at memory of her first love letter.

Totally unaware of surveillance by her family, Shannon's eyes eagerly scanned Monty's bold scrawl:

"Dear Shannon: I've thought of you a lot since I reached Nashville. I've had a lot of time to think while waiting to see people in the music business, mostly on Sixteenth Avenue— "Music Row" they call it here, where record companies, agents, etc. have taken over stately old homes and turned them into studios. Through a guy I know in the business, I got a gig in the Bluebird, a famous old place where a lot of singers have started. I got a surprisingly good response for an amateur, but nothing since. I know it may take years-maybe never. Like any creative career, it's all in just getting the break that gives me a showcase for whatever talent I may have. Keeping my confidence up enough to make contacts hasn't been easy.

Maybe part of the reason behind this is my feeling that I disappointed you badly. I can't say I blame you; I know I chickened out pathetically in the cave. Not a pretty sight! I still cringe when I think about it. This may sound like some lame excuse to you, but I think I mentioned to you about being attacked by a pit bulldog as a kid, torn up enough to spend days in the hospital. I know it's ridiculous, but any dog attack still turns me into a basket case.

My dad and my uncle are probably still laughing over an encounter I had with Uncle Frank's hunting hounds just before I left. Probably everyone around Boxley is still laughing about it, but I still can't. Dad always tried to kid me out of this fear. He bought a guard dog for the horses, thinking I'd get over my phobia. I didn't but I just made damn sure Dad didn't know I was afraid. My dad, the bull rider, just isn't into raising a chicken son! (He wouldn't have been as compassionate as you were if he'd seen me roosting like a big yellow chicken on that ledge of rock in the cave.) I feel like I'm running fever ever time I think of that.

To be very honest, thinking about the first time I kissed you gives me an even higher temp, but it brings a lovely picture of you that lights up my days—and nights.

I'm still giving myself guilt trips too about not telling the sheriff what we knew about Connie's disappearance. I saw something in the Nashville paper last week about Satanic cult and drug activities in the Ozarks. The article reported that hippies were squatting on people's land in the Jasper area, planting pot and booby-trapping the patches to ward off the law as well as the owners of the land. Dad wrote that he ran a bunch off the ranch with his shotgun last week. I'm afraid that's what we blundered into and that Connie and Randy may have gotten sucked in.

Do you think this is possible? I agree with you about the power of evil. I have to admit another thing to you that shames me more than anything else I've told you about myself. I really didn't level with you about what I found in Skull Cave after Gus got hurt. When I went around the corner to where old FOU had been, there was blood all around a burnt-out fire. Back under the shelf where the skeleton had been was a pair of bloody panties, large enough to fit Connie. It finished freaking me out; I just couldn't tell you. So I hid them in the burlap bag I brought back for the dog's head. I also found an old saddlebag, moldy with age, that had a soldier's wallet and tintype pictures like they started making during Civil War Days. Folded in the old wallet is a letter to this soldier's sweetheart, apparently written just before he died when he realizes he will never see her again in this world. His words are lovely enough for a lyric. Maybe I relate so to them, because my feelings were of farewell the last time I looked at you. I felt as if my cowardice likely had cost Gus his life and me---the woman that embodies all the qualities I've dreamed of.

I try to excuse myself by rationalizing that I'm protecting my family by not reporting FOU to the authorities. But to tell you the truth, I think the evil hypnosis of that man, his vow, and his blood still affects me.

I'd love to have your reading on this. You seem much more mature than most girls I've encountered. Am I just a superstitious hillbilly, after all, conjuring up boogers to scare myself in the dark? It gets very dark here in Nashville where I can't bask in the light of your smile. I hope you will write me. Love, Monty."

Shannon sat there visualizing him through layers of tears. When she looked up and saw her parents watching, she turned and gazed out over the meadows, whose pastoral tranquility always soothed. Black and white Holsteins grazed the lush meadows along the Kings River with their spring crop of frisky calves. But, today, she saw only Monty's dark eyes, filled with pain. *I wasn't mistaken; he was saying "goodbye" to me and his life here the last time I saw him. Maybe, that's the only way he can find the courage he must have to succeed.*

Later, when she sat down to write him, her first sentence was: "If you knew me well, you'd know I'm incapable of judgmental love. I love people just as they are, warts and all, just as I hope to be loved someday..."

She stopped writing, picturing the charming, self-deprecating, funny Monty, always the southern gentlemen, deeply caring about everyone but himself. *He can't truly love me until he learns to love himself,* she thought sadly, signing the short note.

CHAPTER XX

Shannon monitored the arrival of mail on her rural route long after common sense warned of the futility of hearing from Monty. On a June morning a year after his graduation and departure for Nashville, restlessness drove her to uncharacteristic action.

Her older brother, Keith, watched her stare morosely out the window while drying a glass repeatedly at the sink. As he walked by on the way to help his father mow a pasture, he flipped her cinnamon-colored pony-tail.

"Take my jalopy if you wanta visit your friends today," he suggested. "Dad swears you're a better driver than any of his sons. . ."

"Well, he didn't seem to think so when I had to tow him on his old tractor last week," she replied glumly. "Didn't even say thanks for all those free chiropractic adjustments I gave him."

As Keith strode out laughing, an idea possessed her. *I'll drive over to Boxley and see what I can find out about Monty.* Her usual self control cautioned: don't be an idiot. *He's forgotten all about you now that he's got a song on the charts. A famous young star doesn't need to be reminded of his failures, and that's all he associates with you. Now that Missy followed him to Nashville, she's probably keeping him too busy to be tempted by all those man-hungry female fans.* But the more her mind tried to dissuade her, the more some inner force manipulated her physically, propelling her to dash in to change into the green dress Monty had loved. She kicked away the faded jeans as she donned the high heels her mother had bought for her seventeenth birthday in an effort to lift Shannon's depression. Now, as she twirled in front of the mirror on her door, making the circular skirt dance, she admitted that looking better lifted her spirits. She felt a twinge of guilt as she penned a hasty note to her mother saying, "I'm going to visit friends—be back when I get back." *That's what she's been urging me to do, isn't it? Yes, but she'd pitch a ninny-fit if she caught you chasing a guy. But you're only seeking news of him. However, feeling this compelling drive to visit Boxley on the very morning when Keith offers his car probably means this is destiny and you will see Monty!* Her excitment became almost as intense as had been her previous depression.

Her spirits soared ahead of the speeding convertible as she raced through Kingsville and began the long climb to the zenith of Magic Mountain. A kaleidoscope of scenes with Monty filled her with wonder at the beauty around and within her. *No more haunting self-doubts, of nightmares and feelings of being possessed.* You've finally matured enough to follow your destiny, she decided smugly. *Today, you're using womanly intuition. Probably that good-ole-boy matter-of-factmess and passive behavior urged by my brothers kept me from competing with Missy for Monty's love.*

Fecund forest smells awakened her senses, and she imagined Monty's long fingers caressing her cheeks like the spring breezes that rippled her flaming banner of hair. In what seemed like minutes rather than hours, she glimpsed the Flying "V" Ranch in the Buffalo River Valley below her. Pulling into a fragrant roadside patch of Mayapple surrounded by blossoning redbud and dogwood, she ran to a flying buttress of stone to see if Monty's pickup might be visible around the house or corrals. The place appeared deserted except for mares and foals cavorting in the nearby meadows. She fought her insane yearning to drive down into the valley and ask Monty's mother about him. Probably Missy already did that many times, she admitted, and most modern girls would do it without thinking twice. Shameless hussies! There you go, boring and prudish. No wonder he lost interest. As she wrestled with the idea of going to the Flying "V", she found herself nearing the Boxley Store and pulled in for a soft drink.

As she sank down on a bench by an old wood stove, a tall old man turned from kidding with a youngster about buying pop bottles. Hitching his seer-sucker trousers over his pot-belly by pulling on red suspenders, he grinned. His twinkling dark eyes under bushy brows reminded her of Monty as he asked, "And who might you be, young lady? Thought I knowed everbody in these parts." He extended his hand. "I'm Frank Villines. Can I get you something?"

"Oh, no. Just stopped for a coke. I'm Shannon Villines." Gulping over her embarrassing fauz pas, she blushed and added hurriedly, looking around to be sure no one else heard, "Um, I mean Shannon Ceranda. I've heard Monty speak of you and his Aunt Opal a lot." *Maybe he'll tell me what's going on with Monty. . .*

Frank slapped his leg. "Well, I'll be dogged. Shoulda knowed ole Monty would know a ravishing little redhead like you if she lived within a hunnerd miles of here." As the implications of Monty's conquests sank into Shannon's subconscious, he went on. "Me'n my missus been invitin' ole Monty to come visit, but I reckon he's had his work cut out for him travelin' with his band and bus, y'know."

"You don't happen to have his address and telephone number, do you?" she asked hesitantly. "I might call and congratulate him."

Just happen to have 'er rightcheer," Frank cackled, raring back and pulling on his suspenders as he studied her face. "Doggone, if that boy is as much a chip offa Uncle Frank's block as I think he is, he wouldn't let his shirttail touch him until he got in touch with you." Hurrying behind the littered counter, he ripped a poster from the wall, a wonderful likeness of Monty with his autograph and address on it. "I won't miss it among all this clutter," he said eyeing the wall-full of yellowed signs advertising everything from snuff to World War I War Bonds. "Sides, he sent my Opal one from his last concert. Reckon that boy still feels bad about lettin' my little Opal-dumplin' git dog-bit 'fore he left."

"I heard about that," she said. "Did the bite cause her much trouble?"

He snapped his adams apple with a bowtie, chuckling. "Naw, in fact, it left the purtiest dimple you ever laid eyes on!" His shoulders and belly seemed synchronized to his laughter. "But, I reckon ole Monty told you my little Opal ain't much on flashin' them dimples of hern at me—let alone at strangers!" He slapped his thigh and laughed so hard he had to wipe sweat from his face with the garter-shortened sleeve of his starched white shirt.

Before Shannon had stopped laughing, the store-owner looked fixedly out the open front door at a vehicle that had pulled into his parking area. He peered over his hornrims, then removed them and cleaned them with his other sleeve as if he could not believe his eyes. Shannon's gaze followed his open-mouthed study of the battered old hearse that crept into the dusty area in front of the weathered, false-fronted frame building.

"Jumpin' Jehorsiefats!" he exclaimed. "If it ain't that doggoned weirdo I been hearin' about. Gotta be that hippie goo-roo that's been messin' up the minds of lots of our hill folks around here."

Shannon's skin rippled with chills as she followed Frank doorward. Sure enough, MostHi FOU sat behind the steering wheel, wearing a purple turban and dark glasses. She glanced around hurriedly for a hiding place if the big Sikh headed inside.

"Wonder what the hell he wants," Frank Villines muttered. "If he wants gas, he can pump it hisself." He stared hard at the old hearse. "I been hearn' how he keeps a baby casket in the back of that meat wagon of his with a baby strung up over it by the neck," he said angrily. "I though some of these fellers must be stringin' ole Frank along, but just lookit that!"

"Is he an undertaker?" Shannon quavered, peering around the door facing, hiding from FOU's view. "What is he doing here?"

"Hellfar, he don't do nuthin' but probly sell drugs and Lord knows what else." Frank exploded. "We oughta run his sorry hindend outa this country." He looked shamefaced. "We would 'ceptin we're scairt spitless of what he might do. That furrin feller's got hisself a gang of white trash capable of any kind of meanness. Houses been burned, livestock stole belongin' to folks who crossed him."

Staring hard at the back of the hearse, Shannon whispered, "Thank God, it's not a real baby, just a baby doll." Then she glimpsed a flash of blond hair from the passenger-side of the old hearse, almost obscured by FOU's height and bulk. "Oh, Lord, who is that with him?" she asked, holding her breath for the answer although she felt she already knew.

"Why, it's that pore little Coger gal from over Kingsville way," Frank said. "You know ole "Shine" Coger's girl. Somebody told me she don't weigh no more'n a washin' of soap since that pervert got a-holt of her. I understand she uset to be a fine figger of a woman. Pore young'n never had a dog's chanct."

Shannon backed out of sight behind the door frame. Picking up a cardboard fan that read "Rooster Snuff", she fanned herself to ward off the faintness. Frank looked puzzled as the old hearse pulled away without either occupant even opening its doors.

"Wonder what he's lookin' fer?" Frank said. "Probably something to steal."

Shannon dropped down on the bench and had another coke while waiting for her legs to become steady enough to carry her back to Keith's convertible. Then, she drove as if pursued, peering into logging roads that intersected the highway to be sure no hearse lurked. Once again, she feared she must be walking a high wire between sanity and possession. The question hounded her: *Can it be his evil blood pounding through your veins that drove you to make this trip today?* I must let Monty know that FOU does have Connie and that she's in desperate shape, she decided driving as fast as the spiraling road down the mountains would permit.

In Kingsville, she rushed into the old store that had been on the square for a hundred years to use the telephone. The owner proceeded to tell her a story about fooling the local man who kept pestering them about when the first telephone would be ready by allowing the poor man to put his head into the sack on a seeder and turn the handle, yelling at the top of his lungs. Unable to appear rude to the white-haired owner that she had known since childhood, she tried to appear attentive to the oft-told story, even doing a phoney chuckle at its end. Then, she learned the telephone was out of order. Peeling out of Kingsville with a squall of tires that brought a head out every door in sight, she defied all the speed laws to race home.

Reaching her house out of breath from dashing up the stairs, she felt grateful that she was still alone in the house as she dialed Monty's number in Nashville. "Bullet Studios," answered a well-modulated voice. But when she asked to speak to Monty Villines or at least get his home number, she was informed that Mr. Villines was on tour and had an unlisted number that could be given to no one.

"But it's an emergency," she pleaded.

"Sorry, miss. No exceptions," the receptionist cooed.

I should've known Monty would get an unlisted number and take all precautions to cut himself off forever from anyone or anything that reminded him of failure in his past, she told herself grimly. The last thing he wants to hear about is Connie, Randy, Gus—or me. Tears dripped from her chin and she did not bother to wipe them away.

Savagely, she grabbed the poster that Frank Villines had given her and wadded it into a big ball which she threw at her wastebasket. "See how you like being thrown away, Mister Bigshot," she yelled childishly.

Overwhelmed by loneliness at loss of her dream, she dashed to the balcony to see if her father and Keith were still mowing. At sight of an old black hearse creeping by on the highway below her house, she clutched her mouth as if her heart might jump out. Then an emaciated arm extended from the rolled-down window on the passenger side, and a long-nailed finger pointed upward to where she stood. Chills chased each other over her like icy-footed rats as she stood riveted to the spot until the hearse left.

"Connie!" she finally croaked. "She's after me for abandoning her!" *She'll make sure that fiend gets me too. How did they know I was at the Boxley Store? Have they been stalking me all the time? Oh God, maybe there is as much power in his blood as he claimed. Otherwise, how did he make me desert all my principles and go over there today?*

Paranoia possessed her with such force that her legs felt like noodles. She sank to her bed, unable to stand. Finally, she regained enough strength to rise and lock her door. Then she fell back on the canopied bed, sobbing and quivering. She tore the ruffled shams from her pillows and covered her head with them to muffle her sobs.

When this tempest of emotion began to subside, she reached from the covers and retrieved Monty's poster. Smoothing his picture out on the coverlet, she accused him wildly of leaving her to face MostHi FOU alone.

Until someone knocked repeatedly on the door, she did not return to reality and realize how far over the edge she had ventured. For a second, she froze, her mind flashing menacing pictures of the giant guru outside her door. Then her mother's gentle voice inquired, "You O.K, Shanny? Who are you talking to?" Her voice became alarmed, "Let me in," she pleaded. When her usually serene mother bagan pounding the door and screaming for help, Shannon tottered to the door.

CHAPTER XXI

Almost two years had passed since Connie Coger's disappearance. Among the superstitious settlers of the remote hills and hollows around Kingsville and Boxley, whispers of animal mutilations and grave robberies circulated. Although rumors surfaced occasionally in Kingsville as to Connie's whereabouts, even her family seemed to assume that she and Randy had simply left the area.

On a Sunday evening, marking the second anniversary of Connie and Randy's induction into MostHi FOU's cult, a feast and orgy had been planned at the cult's hide-out in the Devil's Den Area near Harrison, Arkansas.

MostHi FOU's temple sat far back in a narrow dark canyon and could be approached only by a one-way tunnel through the briar overgrown thickets and trees of FOU's six hundred-forty-acre domain. The two-story temple, trimmed with ornate metallic lace, appeared to be composed of stone pyramids with their tops lopped off, each topped by a smaller triangle-shaped structure. Front shelves on the strange structure held statues of copulating couples, some in six-nine positions. The top of the temple had a church spire topped by a wrought iron pentagram. Over the heavy entry door appeared the name "GURDWARA" which was framed by a border of intertwined vipers.

Almost obscuring the temple of FOU towered a taller pyramid, facing the narrow approach tunnel. This flat-topped pyramid held an open grave, whose headstone read in large engraving, "HERE LIES JESUS CHRIST, KING OF THE JEWS." Inside the open casket lay a very realistic replica of the crucified Christ which looked as if it might have come from the altar of a Catholic church.

Much of the terrain in the Devil's Den region became impassable before white settlement when an earthquake scrambled precipices, mountains and river beds, leaving rock slides, laying foot-wide crevices through geologic formations and tilting others. Countless caverns ran through the limestone formations, abandoned and dark after the river had its course changed by the quake.

Jack Baadshaw and a dozen of his cohorts, recruited from the nearby mountains, had just returned from raiding the nearby Ozark Wildlife Club the night before the feast. An exclusive hunting club that flew millionaires in to hunt every thing from wild boars to trophy animals, this refuge had provided provender for the cult's poachers as well as a market for some of their illicit drug sales.

Jed Baadshaw led Hank, his nearly blind brother, inside. Connie Coger sat at a table as the men boasted and argued over who had made the biggest haul during the hunt. Although a cup of steaming coffee sat nearby, Connie ignored the drink as well as most of the loud boasting, staring into space or putting her head on the table. The girl was so thin, she appeared emaciated. Her sunken eyes looked out hopelessly over dark smudges, and her pallor had a purplish cast. Neglect showed in greasy, lank hair and grungy dungarees.

The long tables in the temple's large kitchen were stacked with gutted animals: deer, wild boar, turkeys and smaller game, even a few squirrels. When the Baadshaws revved up a chain saw and began carving up the deer, they spewed blood on the floor and spattered Connie's bowed head, but she did not appear to notice at first. When she raised her head, she looked at the gore and clapped a fragile hand over her mouth, rising quickly to run outside to vomit. Hank watched her go, through glasses resembling bottle bottoms.

"That gal don't stop doin' drugs an start eatin', she gonna die!" Hank Baadshaw predicted solemnly, spitting sloppily toward a spittoon in the kitchen's corner. "She go 'round in a trance, too spaced out to eat."

"You a fine one to talk," his bearded brother remarked. "Mosta the time you're so blasted you can't find your own A-hole. Way you missin' that there spittoon, yore eyesight musta done totally left you." Hank eyed him with his bluish-gray pupils, then slapped him with a bloody hand.

"Stop it, you bloody bastard!" Jed Baadshaw yelled, brandishing the knife he was using to castrate the wild boar being prepared for roasting in an open pit behind the temple. "Maybe if you eat these boar nuts it'll restore your sight as well as your manhood." He flung the bloody genitals in his brother's face, then ran away with Hank chasing him—falling over everything in his path.

When Connie regained enough strength, she walked to the temple steps and sank down to rest. Suddenly, the ear-shattering roar and flatulations of many engines filled the air. Connie felt too far from reality to be more than mildly surprised as twenty motorcycles wheeled into the hollow, most of them carrying leather-clad men with women on the sissy-bars behind them. The riders killed their Harley Davidsons. At sight of Connie on the temple steps, one of the bearded men dismounted quickly and rushed over to her. Not until he shouted, "Connie, it's Munro!" did she recognize her older brother. Reeking of moonshine, he grabbed her and swung her around.

"Doggoned, if you don't look like you did as a kid," he chortled, obviously surprised at her loss of weight. "These here guys are friends of mine," he said with a sweep of his hand toward the motorcycles. "Most of 'em are Hells Angels from Californy."

As the cyclists dismounted and surrounded Connie, Munro shouted,

"See, guys! I told you I knowed FOU's ole lady!'

One of the rough-looking riders strode around looking over the temple and layout. Removing the red bandanna from around his mop of long hair, he wiped sweat. "You shore you're not just bullin' about what this dude can get us?" he demanded suspiciously, scratching his privates. "Damn, I'm gallded as hell. That 'hog' of mine turned into a damn razorback when I roared across the Arkansas line!"

"Hell no. Where's ole Randy?" Munro asked Connie. "He can tell you. He invited us here and has already made arangements with FOU."He shook Connie as she sat there looking dazed. "I ast you where ole Randy is," her brother demanded.

Lackluster eyes reflected her deep depression. At first, she sulled, then said, "Aw, off somewhere with MostHi FOU getting ready for tonight's worship feast," Connie showed no surprise or gladness at seeing her relative. He took her by the shoulders and shook her again.

"What in hell's wrong with you, girl? You ack like you're retarded. Did you even know our paw died not long after you runned off?"

She shook her head indifferently, still looking confused.

Munro yelled "Hell, we'd a let you know about the funeral if you'd a let a body know where you was." The bandannaed biker remounted restlessly, raced his motor to remind Munro of the group irritation.

"I wouldn't a come if I'd known," she declared angrily. "I'm glad the bastard is dead." For the first time her face registered emotion, becoming purple—splotched from anger.

"Well, he got hisself stabbed in a fight with ole Hankins over that still at Center Point. I'd a gone after Hankins, but I sorta figgered he done a service to us an humanity."

The gallded biker was again pacing circles around them walking wide. "Lissen, Man, my guys are gettin' restless," he told Munro. "You gotta either put up or shut up." He turned on Connie. "Your brother invited us here. Claimed ole FOU got speed, pot an a lotta other goodies to spice up our nights." His eyebrows did a suggestive little dance, and he pretended to twirl tassels on his hairy chest. "Is he just bullin?"

Connie's stomach did slow rolls getting a whiff of him. As Connie maintained a sullen silence, Munro grabbed her wrists and twisted until she winced.

"Is ole Randy Rat lyin'? Tole me to bring these guys here and he and FOU would fix us up. Claims he's got pot and pussy galore. Regular hog-heaven for bikers!"

She fought her nausea to answer. "No, he ain't lying. They'll be back shortly. Go 'round in back and ask Hank Baadshaw." When he released her, she disappeared inside the temple.

CHAPTER XXII

The Hell's Angels maintained the silence requested by MostHi FOU as he sat on the raised throne at the front of the domed sanctuary. Today, FOU wore a purple Sikh-style turban with a large Cat's Eye stone holding its folds so that only the crimson tatoo of the dragon's tongue showed between his flashing dark eyes. His black cape had wedge-shaped cuneiform writing in gold down its front. On the left breast of his Nehru-style black tunic shone a circle pen of huge luminous pearls with a cross of star rubies resembling tears of blood. The front of his loin cloth was fastened with a glittering diamond Pentagram, and his gold sandals gleamed with precious stones.

The eyes of most of the rough spectators glittered with anticipation of FOU's heralded orgy and feast. Munro had further whetted the sensual appetites of the Hell's Angel motorcyclists by describing scenes Randy had promised of drugs, incredible perversions, and drunken carousal.

However, when Connie Smith approached the throne, walking like a sleepwalker, nude except for a transparent chiffon gown bound beneath her large breasts with a golden tasseled cord, one of the girl bikers shouted an obscenity. Fixing the drunken harasser with his piercing eyes, MostHi FOU silenced the slovenly drunk. Then he pointed with a long-nailed finger to the door, and the heckler's companion hustled her out.

Clapping his hands together before his face, he brought total silence to the assemblage; then he bowed and his rich voice fell over the crowd like black velvet. Bowing deeply, he said, "Salaam Memsahibs, Salaam Sahibs! Rom Rom Alecum!"

"He means 'Howdy'," the nearly sightless Hank Baadshaw interpreted with a wraparound smile on his broad face that made him resemble a bullfrog. He rose, bowed toward MostHi FOU, then motioned for the crowd to follow suit. As he turned to fumble his way back to his seat, one of his brothers tripped him, guffawing drunkenly until MostHi FOU's eyes commanded silence once more.

Randy Smith slouched on the front bench beside Connie's brother. . . appearing quiet and withdrawn. Pale and unshaven, he seemed to have lost his former bravado. When he tried to bow following Hank's example, he would have fallen to the floor had Munro Coger not caught him by the ponytail and shoved him back with a big hand against Randy's narrow chest.

Fixing the crowd with his hypnotic eyes, MostHi FOU proclaimed in his powerful voice: "All of the men gathered here except the motorcycle club are blood brothers with me, MostHi Father of the Universe, and partakers of the power I am able to confer. All my blood brothers will never die. Each has power to overcome any obstacle the world puts in his path.

"Many centuries ago, people in India learned how to train elephants so that a puny man could control beasts weighing tons. Newborn elephants were tied to a tree with a large rope. In a few days, the elephant learned that tugging against a tree was useless. Soon, as the elephant grew, a small stake held him. To this day, these gigantic animals, capable of easily uprooting the largest tree, stay tied to a string on a peg. This is called learned helplessness.

"I tell you, men, your churches and government trained you to be helpless in the same way by making you fear puny laws and religious rules that should never limit powerfully potential potentates you can become. Through the centuries, certain men have learned to plug themselves into my power: men like the Mafia who take all the money, sex and power they want without fear.

"MostHi Father of the Universe will now demonstrate to all of you this power available to my subjects. Please step forward, Brother Hank Baadshaw."

Hank had become obese as his vision waned. Fluid had built an apron of fat that almost touched his knees. His ankles bloused over his shoes. One bare ankle looked gangrenous. As Hank stumbled over a biker's feet in the aisle, his brother, Jack, stepped forward and assisted him to the front of the temple. Taking the big man's overall galluses, Jack guided his nearly-blind brother up the three steps leading to the low platform below MostHi FOU's throne.

"As you observe, brethren," the cult leader continued, "Brother Hank is almost blind from Diabetes. I propose to allow my brother to partake of self-immolation in which the old body consumes itself with fire and is replaced by a later model, free of blindness and disease." MostHi FOU rose and stood with arms outstretched over Hank Baadshaw's wooly head.

As everyone held their breaths in apparent awe, the silence seemed absolute. Into this silence, Randy's shrill voice inquired irritably: "What the devil's goin' on? Hellfar, why's it so quiet?" He stood, weaving visibly and looking wildly around. "Hell, git the show on the road." One trouser leg was secured with a bikers chain.

"I see Brother Randy wishes to participate also," FOU drawled icily, flashing his barricuda smile. "This shall be his penance for getting so drunk he does not know better than to take my name in vain. Stand him here beside Brother Hank, Jack." Hank's lantern-jawed younger brother carried the slight Randy Smith and set him on the stage near Hank, where he promptly sprawled at FOU's feet. The room became suddenly black as night, and FOU's powerful voice focused every eye on him.

"MostHi Father of the Universe now commands that the darkness consume these two men and allow them to burst into light to guide the footsteps of others in this temple." With explosive bursts of brilliance, two flaming figures materialized. The bikers gasped, stopping their swearing exclamations when the lights came on, revealing only two mounds of ashes where the men had stood on the stage. Randy's chain lay beside one mound.

"What in the—," exclaimed Munro Coger, stopping, himself, and gazing in slack-mouthed wonder to where the eight-foot Father of the Universe towered over even the largest of the Baadshaws.

"Know that MostHi Father of the Universe has the power to consume any of you—all of you—to return you to the dirt from whence you came," MostHi FOU bellowed, his eyes narrowing menacingly. "I give this power to each of you for the asking, demanding only in return that you vow allegiance to me with a blood oath."

"How many of you have seen Jesus Christ or God perform even one such miracle here on earth?" His eyes roved the room, and the biker's eyes refused to meet his compelling gaze. "Even your Bible confessed that God feared my power and banished me from Heaven. But we can establish our own kingdom here, much better than any dull, moral place paved with gold!"

Then MostHi FOU extended his arms over the two piles of ashes where Hank Baadshaw and Randy Smith had been. Lights dimmed and total blackness reigned while FOU chanted an incantation in an unknown tongue. Suddenly, lighted outlines of two men emerged on stage. Then the dome of the temple glowed like the night firmament filled with exploding rockets that showered stars on the awestruck crowd. Connie Smith lay on the altar, golden hair touching the floor.

When the lights came on, many of the spectators knelt by their benches, wide-eyed and pale at the sight of Hank Baadshaw and Randy Smith, both leaping about the stage and praising the MostHI.

"I can see!" shouted Hank, gazing at his hands like a child at first discovery. "Praise Most High! I am well; I can see!" Hank's four hundred pound body floated across the stage, feather-like, as he leaped and shouted.

Randy cried, "Praise be!" as he soared over the altar where Connie still lay as if asleep.

As Baadshaw and Smith danced through the crowd, MostHi FOU stood over the altar, staring down at Connie until silence was restored.

"Certain women are privileged to learn of me how to bring joy and sensual pleasure to many men," he murmured, bending to caress Connie. "Through the centuries, such women have borne the fruit of my loins to re-populate the world with men who are not lower than the angels, but who share with the Gods all the wealth, power and love the world has to offer. To you women in the temple, I offer the same opportunity Connie has embraced.

"My people, both men and women, cannot be hurt by anything the world can marshal against them. My people are bullet-proof, fire-proof, totally indestructible--immortal in every sense of the word. . .

"You may take the blood oath and gain immortality, or you may become small heaps of ashes in this room, to be swept out with the other rubbish by my men." His gaze darted like lightning from one face to the other of the bikers, lingering on those who seemed ready to bolt. "Lock the doors, Jack!" he commanded. "But first, go outside and bring the couple in that I banished. No witnesses to your destruction can remain." As soon as the couple were ushered back into the temple, the double doors were securely barred.

"Line up at the side aisle to take the blood oath," MostHi FOU ordered. The bearded cyclists looked at MostHi FOU, at the laden tables of food, at the naked girl on the altar, at each other, then began to line up. Even the drunken girl and her escort meekly got in line.

MostHi FOU stood over the altar, slowly removing his loin cloth, making the tatooed serpent extend and retreat as Connie's pelvis began to rotate letting the shadow of the thrusting viper tongue fall across her pale face. Taking a jewel-studded scimitar from its sheath, he flicked the chiffon of Connie's robe away from her left breast. The awe-struck observers began to gasp as blood bubbled up like a fountain from its rosy aureole.

"Men, you may share my blood at this fountain," MostHi FOU directed with a gesture toward Connie. "This woman is one with me because of her blood oath; therefore, you partake of my blood through her."

"I'll be the first to receive the sacrament," Munro Coger said hurriedly, obviously afraid that MostHi FOU might expect him to object.

But as Munro bent over his sister to drink, MostHi FOU stretched out on the altar beside her, baring his own left breast, from which blood began to spout.

"Perhaps the women would prefer to take their sacrament from me," he suggested, willing the first biker woman to approach with his commanding eyes as he stroked himself.

CHAPTER XXIII

The switchboard operator at the television station in North-west Arkansas said cheerily, "Good Afternoon! This is Channels twenty-nine and forty, KHOG-TV. May I help you?" Listening, she waited. "Yes, I'll connect you with Mike Conroy, our News Director in that area."

Mike Conroy picked up the telephone on his newsroom desk at the Fort Smith television affiliate.

"Hello! I'm Mike Conroy. What may I do for you?" He listened a second, half raising from his seat in perceptible shock. "What's that again? Most high WHAT?" Grabbing a yellow pad, he wrote hurriedly, trying to slow the caller down with countless, "Would you repeat that?" and other delaying questions.

"Um, yes, Mister—uh—Most High Father, I understand, I guess...But if this suicide is planned in Jasper, why do you desire publicity? Oh, um, I see—this couple is to die and be—resurrected—so that the world will recognize your—um—sovereign power. Um—sir—this all sounds—well—sorta famil-iar—like from the Bible, you know, only—wel—sorta weird. You sure this isn't a practical joke? Your voice sounds like that ole George whatchamacallit, that Limey dude in Fayetteville."

The caller's voice became so loud that Mike held the tele-phone away from his ear. Tapping his hornrims on the yellow pad, he waited.

"Well, Sir, you understand why I might think this is a crank call, Sir," he said, beginning to write once more. "And you say this suicide pact is to be enacted tomorrow morning about seven at the Highway Seven Bridge at the Jasper city limits. That's the highway coming in from Harrison? Right? You sure you mean Jasper, Arkansas? Why that little town looks like Peace personified!"

The line went dead, and the newsman scratched his head, trying to decide whether to check with the Little Rock and Fayetteville newsrooms and be the butt of a practical joke or dismiss this as a prank.

I'd better check it out. Something about that guy's English accent and deep voice. The ring of authority. Maybe it's the English accent, but I'd better see if the Jasper police know anything about this. He shivered as he dialed the Jasper number.

CHAPTER XXIV

Two years of heady climb to fame as a singer-songwriter in Nashville had changed Monty Villines very little outwardly. He still wore faded denim and boots, lived in the same old place near sixteenth. Watching his songs become hits that bulleted to the tops of contemporary as well as country-western charts proved exhilirating, yet he remained essentially the small town boy without a great deal of self-confidence and poise. With most of his time booked for country-wide tours, Monty found no time for himself. His old pickup turned balky from neglect, so he grabbed a studio limo for seldom needed local transportation.

When "Twilight Time" bulleted up the charts for weeks, his time in Nashville became all recording sessions and personal appearances. An RCA recording contract allowed him to purchase his own bus for a nation-wide tour of personal appearances. But the biggest thrill of being a so-called Nashville "star" came when he sent his father the money to postpone selling the ranch. His father's appreciative note became a cherished keepsake in the celebrity scrapbook he had started collecting for the time after this incredible bubble of fame dissipated.

On a Thursday afternoon in early June, 1977, Monty sat in the waiting room of the Bullet Recording Studio, waiting for the members of his band to arrive for a recording session. Nursing a hangover, he cursed himself for indulgences at last night's concert in Dallas. He still could not believe the bevy of beauties waiting at every appearance, willing to do anything, for one moment with a celebrity. When the gorgeous Dallas model knocked on his dressing room door, his producer had yelled, "Another one ready to trip ole Monty, and beat him to the floor."

He had just finished talking with his friends from OSU, Scott Hendricks and Tim DuBois, producers of the meteoric Restless Heart group, and felt encouraged by Songwriter DuBois' comments about his lyrics. Tim, who had written for most of the stars such as Alabama, Restless Heart and Jerry Reed, particularly liked Twilight Time.

"That one will get the bullet the day it's released," Tim had predicted confidently to Monty's great satisfaction. He tried to think of that as he waited, feeling terribly restless and lonely in the smoke-filled room. His mind kept running videos of Shannon, the light in those glowing eyes as he had recited *Twilight Time* for her. I'm glad I dedicated it to her on the album, he thought, even though she's probably engaged or married by now. He squirmed at the thought that he had not answered her letter. *A girl that lovely and young probably is seriously involved with someone else by now.* Just thinking about her still gave him a set-back on the battle he had been waging to increase his self-esteem and poise for stage appearances.

But she did write that she never loved conditionally. She didn't say she loved you—unconditionally or any other way. Forget it, he told himself, wiping away the tears caused by allergy to the heavy tobacco smoke in the waiting room. He looked at his Timex watch. *The damned thing had stopped.* You should've bought yourself a watch and a pickup instead of going in debt for that bus, he thought, groaning inwardly as he thought of the expensive work needed on his Nineteen-Sixty-Five Chevy pickup.

Most of the time offstage, Monty felt rootless, with no time to return home, to renew ties there, regain his identity. He related to the Rhinestone Cowboy in the Glen Campbell song: a "lotta compromisin' on the way to my horizon" for sure, he thought, trying to recall how many drinks got him on stage in Dallas. And how many pills put him to sleep afterward. Those things blurred on the road—along with the gorgeous girls offering young bodies for a moment in fame's spotlight.

Approaching the Bullet receptionist, he asked her to tell his band he would be back shortly. His ears still rang from the mind-bending volume of his last concert. The girl gave him the eye and repeated her assurances of willing servitude.

Then he headed for his pickup, planning to take it to a shade-tree mechanic he knew for an estimate. Outside the impressive Bullet Studio, he noticed a newspaper rack and decided to grab a paper to pass the time while the mechanic checked his engine.

As he bent to insert his quarter in the paper dispenser, he read the headline and froze. Dropping the quarter in his nervousness, he knelt by the rack long enough to read: Dateline: Jasper, Arkansas, Thursday, June 2, 1977." Another glance confirmed that Connie Coger Smith indeed figured in the horrible headline he had first glimpsed: ARKANSAS COUPLE ANNOUNCE SUI-

CIDE PACT. He chased the quarter down in the dirty gutter, inserted it, extracted the paper, and let his weak knees lower him to the trash-littered curb.

His eyes scanned so fast that his shocked brain could hardly process the information fed into its computer from the Dallas Morning News front page: "Media representatives at KHOG-TV outlets in Fayetteville, Fort Smith and Little Rock, Arkansas, report requests for television news coverage of a suicide scheduled to be enacted by twenty-two-year-old Connie Coger Smith and twenty-seven-year-old Randolph Smith, formerly of Kingsville, at 7:00 A.M. Friday, June 3, 1977. The caller identified himself to KHOG-TV New Director, Mike Conroy, as "Most High Father of the Universe," claiming that the suicide would take place the following morning on the Highway Seven Bridge leading into the small hamlet of Jasper, Arkansas. News Director Conroy quoted the caller as saying, "Connie and Randy Smith are dying willingly by their own hands after twelve-hundred sixty days of witnessing the power of Most High! Father of the Universe. He will raise them from the dead after three and one-half days, proving that Most High Father of the Universe indeed holds the keys to power in this world and the world to come."

"Fearing the call might be a hoax, Conroy checked with Jasper police officials and found that the pair had stopped a Greyhound bus, pretending to be potential passengers, then taking the driver and ten passengers hostage. At present, the pair have blockaded the Highway Seven Bridge with the bus, threatening to shoot the driver and ten hostages if police interfere before the television crews arrive and have time to cover their suicides.

"The Arkansas State Highway Patrol Headquarters at Little Rock announced dispatch of a police helicopter and SWAT Team to Jasper as soon as they learned of the hostages. Local police, as well as the Newton County Sheriff's Posse are at the scene of the standoff."

"OhmiGod!" wailed Monty, dropping the paper, forgetting everything but his need to try to reach Connie as he long-legged toward his old pickup and headed toward Jasper.

CHAPTER XXV

The Cerandas, Jim, Josephine, and Shannon, stopped in their tracks, spellbound by the television news broadcast at 6:00 P.M. Thursday, June 2, detailing the suicide pact and hostage standoff at Jasper. Josie protested vainly as the impetuous pair grabbed car keys, jackets, purse and headed for Jim's pickup. Gesturing helplessly toward the tableful of steaming food, yet untasted, she was still sputtering as they disappeared down the stairwell from the second story living room.

She even ran to the upper balcony to continue her pleas:

"B--but, Shanny, what can you and Daddy do if Connie won't talk to the police, what chance do you have? And you might get shot! She's undoubtedly c-r-a-z-y. . ." The sound of Jim's tires squalled a protest as he peeled out and headed toward Jasper. Muttering to herself about the "hard-headed pair", she stored the meal in the refrigerator, unable to eat a bite herself due to her anxiety.

"Maybe Jim'll come to his senses and make her come home before bedtime," she murmured with a look upward that turned it into a supplication. These last months of battling Shannon's depression had taken their toll. Sometimes she felt she might end up in Little Rock at the mental hospital herself.

By the time Shannon and her father headed south out of Harrison at a high rate of speed on "Scenic Seven" Highway as advertised by State Tourism, darkness was turning its torturous twists into a daredevil speedway for Jim's drive to arrive and see what was happening. When his tires squalled on a curve, Shannon glanced over the treetops and outcrops below the narrow, snaky curves of the descent toward Jasper and cautioned:

"Better slow 'er down a tad, Parnell! We do want to arrive alive."

"I'm the only one that's supposed to say that," he said grimly, reducing his speed back to the posted limit. Just as he did so, a highway patrol cruiser came into view behind them with siren and lights going, passing at twice the legal speed. "That's what I need, a siren, to finish off my nerves," he commented. "But, I don't need a ticket, so I'm glad I slowed down."

"You know, Mom was probably right," she admitted ruefully. "I likely won't get a chance to even see Connie, but I just have to try." Tempted to reveal to her father the guilt she still felt over not reporting their contact with FOU, she decided the time still was not right as he gradually regained his original rate of speed, gimlet-eyes on the road.

"Maybe at least Connie will see a friendly face in the mob if I'm there," she reasoned as they reached the outskirts of Jasper and were stopped abruptly by an Arkansas Highway Patrol blockade.

Parking their pickup on the roadside, they hiked hurriedly through blocks of law enforcement vehicles, some with radios and lights still going full blast. A couple of times, police stopped them and they were only able to proceed further by explaining that they were friends of the people holding hostages and hoping to intercede to stop the violence.

Shannon's arms rippled with chill bumps as the darkened Greyhound bus came into view. White blurs of faces appeared at the windows on the side facing the north where most of the police were massed.

Shannon's father approached Bill Madden, Newton County Sheriff and a friend. "Any chance we could try to talk to the girl?" Jim asked.

"Hell, no," Madden responded instantly, then looked apologetically at Shannon. "We already tried to get one of Connie's aunts close enough to reason with her neice. Damned if she didn't fire at both of us! Purt nigh scairt the old lady outa her wits. We saw Connie plain when she fired. Face of a crazy woman! Her aunt said she wouldn't of knowed her had she met her in broad daylight. Skinny as a gut with everthing squoze out."

"Oh, God, what has that nut done to her?" Shannon sobbed. "The Connie I knew smiled at everyone—even the worst kind of creeps." Her father patted her awkwardly.

"Yow, probably smiled at one too many when she got involved with ole Randy," the sheriff agreed grimly, adding, "You two are welcome to sit in my Jeep. Looks like we're just going to have to wait this situation out. Try to avoid gettin' innocent people killed if possible. I'd like to git my hands on that nut that's behind this."

"Much obliged," Jim said, helping Shannon into the back

seat of the county vehicle. "Do you know anything about who he is, where he came from or anything?"

'Sheriff Madden shook his big Stetson soberly. "Naw, very little. Claims to be a sorta Indian goo-roo, I hear. Sure don't speak Arkansas worth a durn. Sounds like one a them Britishers. I had him in my jail onct, an he spooked the jailer. Claimed she felt something called an "evil arrow" before she even knowed he was a prisoner. Swore he was conjurin' up spells in that cell all night. I suspected him of peddlin' drugs but could never prove anything."

"Where is he now? Do you know?" Shannon asked.

"He's been makin' hisself scarce as hen's teeth ever since this started," the sheriff replied. "Before that, he was doing some boasting around about having a big convention of his followers from all over the country. I followed a passel of Hell's Angels out to his old hang-out near Devil's Den the other day. But I didn't have no search warrant, so backed off."

Through the long night, Shannon waited, unwilling to leave at her father's urging: "Your mother will be worried sick; we'd better go; we can't do anything."

"I have to stay, dad," she insisted, shivering more from fright than from the cold fog rising from the stream below the bridge. He put her sweater around her shoulders and hugged her, settling back to wait with her.

If only I could see Monty and talk to him about the guilt, she thought miserably. He's probably wiped all memory of the incident in the cave from his mind, all memory of me too now that he's getting well-known. She fought to pull the plug on her mental switchboard when her thoughts returned to the starlit night and their first kiss. Just thinking about it made her feel warm enough to remove the sweater and forget for a few minutes the tragic drama unfolding before their eyes. Surely he could not erase totally the ecstasy of that kiss as they sat in the fragrant bower of apple blossoms feeling one with the firmament blazing above them. His bronzed face became real once again as she closed her eyes to the horror waiting to happen; she felt his muscular body holding her close, heard the murmur of the stream blending into a symphony with the myriad voices from the forest. But agonizing hours of blackness returned.

As Friday's sun sent a few timorous rays over the mountain, Sheriff Madden hopped back into the front seat and reported by radio that the television crews had arrived, spurring some activity in the Greyhound bus.

When Connie Smith appeared at the bus door pushing the gray-clad driver ahead of her at gunpoint, Shannon rubbed the doodads from sleepy eyes to make sure the eyes were working. The blonde holding the gun looked twenty years older than the Connie Coger she had known. Appearing to weigh less than one hundred pounds, the girl had violet crescents under each eye, the appearance of anorexia. Her long unkempt hair fell on her faded chambray workshirt that billowed to the ragged knees of her dirty jeans.

She lifted what appeared to be a police bullhorn to her blue lips and shrieked: "Prepare to record for the world my witness to the supreme power of MostHi Father of the Universe! In fifteen minutes, my brother Randy Smith, also a witness to our father's power, will sacrifice himself with the calm belief that he will return, alive and renewed in body and spirit within three and one-half days at this site. If the police interfere with Randy's witness by suicide, I will not hesitate to shoot this man." She gestured with the gun against the temple of the manacled and blindfolded driver. Although her eyes were maniacal, her speech seemed toneless and robotic. Her Ozarky twang had changed to FOU's stilted English accent.

"When Randy's witness is finished, I will take my own life with this gun to testify to the world of my faith in our MostHi Father of the Universe."

As the television crews and photographers from local newspapers positioned themselves cautiously, Connie urged, using the bullhorn once more:

"Move in close, you cowards! Here is an opportunity for you to learn how to banish all fear. All power is available to each of you by merely acknowledging MostHi FOU as your master. He alone can make each of you impervious to any harm, banish any disease, and resurrect you from death."

Loudspeakers began urging the girl to relase the hostages and surrender.

At this point, Randy emerged from the bus, appearing to be

high on something, acting as cocky and obnoxious as ever. He strutted in front of the cameras, posing, smoothing back his meager Van Dyke beard and tightening the rubber band on his sandy ponytail. As he neared the end of the bus where the hidden SWAT team had asked the television crew to halt, Randy mugged shamelessly, twirling his old German revolver then aiming it toward his own heart. When he lifted the gun high in the air and gave a cowboy yell, the police marksman with a scope fired, sending the Luger spinning back toward Connie and her hostage. Randy spun around and reeled backward, knocking the hostage from in front of Connie, holding his shattered arm before his pale face, blinded by blood and pain. Screaming, he groped blindly for Connie. Picking up the Luger, she calmly pulled Randy's right hand down, placed it around the gun and pulled the trigger, aiming for his heart.

The loud echoes of the explosion had barely died as Randy's body crumpled and the police marksman zeroed in on Connie, bringing her down atop Randy with a hail of bullets.

Pandemonium broke loose as Connie shuddered, then became still. Highway patrolmen and police rushed in to remove the manacles and blindfold from the driver and to free the other jubilant hostages.

CHAPTER XXVI

Monty Villines' old Chevy pickup sputtered and quit for the tenth time within sight of a tiny one-pump service station in the midst of the lovely, remote Ozark National Forest north of Little Rock. The owner's gaunt face lit up when Monty limped under the rickety shelter and slumped down beside him on a bench made out of a split hickory with legs inserted through the bark side.

"Howdy!" the tall mountaineer greeted. "You look sorta petered out. I'm Clell Glanders!" He stuck out a long, greasy hand and Monty pumped it, giving the man his name.

"I left Nashville with a sick pickup," he explained, pulling off his cowboy boots and looking ruefully at the holes in his socks that had sprouted blisters. "I've been doctoring on it all the way up, and I think it just died on me. Walked five miles once for jumper cables."

"What's her symptoms?" Clell inquired, turning his head for a second to aim a squirt of tobacco juice at a wide' crack in the porch. "Do she go clunkenty clunk and then just die?"

"Well, she did once and I had to have her jumped that time," Monty said.

"Hell, I can fix anything 'ceptin these here newuns," the tall station owner drawled, scratching the grizzled stubble on his outthrust chin. He rose, resting his long arms by hooking thumbs in the unbuttoned sides of his faded TufNut overalls, staring at Monty's pickup. "What make 'n model is she?"

Monty told him and 'mimicked the sounds emitted repeatedly by the Chevy several times before it quit.

"Was she sprayin' gas?" the oldtimer inquired, scratching himself.

"Not at first, but I could smell it real strong. Kept thinking it was flooding. Probably made it worse by holding the foot feed down hard.This last time though, it sprayed gas all over the road."

"'Pears like you might need a fuel pump," Clell surmised, obviously thrilled at the thought of a customer.

Why in the world would a man think he could make a living with a service station in this remote area wondered Monty. *He undoubtedly only sees a few tourists in the summer and a few fools like me trying to save time by taking a shortcut.*

"You got one on hand?" Monty asked eagerly.

Clell shifted his cud of tobacco and scratched his gray thatch.

"By dogeys, I ain't got one, but I think they's one that might work on that old wrecked pickup out back. Some feller just give it to me to pull it off the road. So's I'd be glad to give 'er to you and just charge you real cheap fer the labor." He eyed the young man with kindly eyes.

"You got a deal, Man!" Monty yodeled, grabbing the other's bent shoulder. "But I can pay for the part too if it'll work. I've got to get home. I'd even rent a pickup if you've got one so I could go on while you fix mine!"

"I got one," Mr. Glanders said hesitantly, looking down his

long nose at Monty. "But, to tell you the truth, I ain't been able to get 'er to run."

Monty tried not to show his frustration and dwindling expectations. "Well, do the best you can," He began to pace nervous circles.

"You just mind my bizness an I'll go get that fuel pump." Grabbing some tools, the gangly mountaineer headed for the back of the station.

"I don't know if I can handle all these customers," Monty grumbled, grabbing a paper from the station counter and stopping mid-stride to read. The headline read: "POLICE RESCUE HOSTAGES IN JASPER." His fear ran ahead of his eyes. He stumbled outside, gasping for air. As he read the tragic story, he sank down on the bench and bowed his head, not caring that the tears beaded down, tasting salty on his lips.

Clell returned with the used fuel pump dripping in one long hand. Pausing he looked curiously at Monty's face and the discarded newspaper, nervously clearing his throat and fidgeting. Obviously uncomfortable with Monty's display of emotion, he watched as Monty pulled out a handkerchief and wiped tears. "Well, make yourself to home whilst I git yore truck fixed," he said gently. "Hep yourself to some sody pop. I got two in there on the counter. Take whichever one suits yore tastebuds." He hurried away, leaving a trail of muddy tracks and grease spots. "Gotta git this thang in stalls," he muttered as he left.

"Damn, I let fear do it to me again!" Monty kicked angrily at the nearby porch post, forgetting his bootless foot. Although he winced and grabbed his foot, he took a savage pleasure in inflicting the physical pain, as if his accusing mind said, "You deserve it!" *Your fear sentenced Connie to death.*

Your fear cost poor old Gus his life and probably cost you Shannon. Too late for regrets about Gus and Connie. Too late. Too late. Too late for Shannon too. The black curtain of depression dropped over him once more, shutting out any ray of hope. I might as well go back to Nashville and wait for my fame bubble to burst too, his thoughts warned. *I've failed to stand for anything. Smokin', drinkin', messin' around. Learning being in heat pales beside being in love.* Suddenly, his mother's cheery face appeared inside the blackness, her sweet voice saying, "Son, if you forget every thing I ever told you, don't forget this; the Bible says `Fear not' three hundred and sixty-five times, one for each day of the year. Jesus rolled away the hopeless fear like the stone from his tomb" *My bravado never fooled ole mom for a second.*

Jerking the boots on, he rose purposefully and hurried out to help Clell, discovering in short order that Clell knew almost as little as he did about fixing the "olduns" too. Being under a shade tree didn't seem to help either of them as mechanics. But, miraculously, when they were through, the old engine coughed, then started. With renewed hope, Monty let Clell pour gasoline over his hands, washed off the grease, generously paid for the work and gas, then mounted his rusty steed for the home stretch.

"I gotta go home" he muttered, "can't go back to Nashville until I go home and remember just who I really am. I just know that peach-orchard-boar lookin back when I shave is enough to make a cat puke, as my mama would say. For the first time he realized how deeply he yearned for her and home. As he drove, he flipped on the radio. Recognizing the lyrics of his latest release, he turned up the volume of *Twilight Time.*

"Voices of all creatures, blend at twilight time. Their meadow-mountain lullabye soothes earth's children when we cry." *What a masterful job Scott had done on the sound. And Tim had showed him the way to turn poetry into lyrics.* He pictured Shannon's face as he read her the lyrics, and his heart bounced at the thought of seeing her.

For the first time, he recalled his band waiting in Nashville, probably mounting a manhunt for him by now. He hit the brakes, spewing gravel. Then he shrugged, and peeled out thinking: I'll call them and suggest they take some time with their loved ones like I hope to...

For the first time, he realized also that he had not looked at the dateline on the paper he read at the station. He found himself feeling grateful at the probability of Connie and Randy's funerals being behind him.

CHAPTER XXVII

Shannon began sobbing uncontrollably as she approached the small chapel and cemetery in the mountains near Kingsville. Her father reached over to hug her awkwardly while her mother joined in her sobs. Through the tears, Shannon noticed a throng of people around the mobile home on the mountain side now occupied by Connie Smith's brother since their father's violent death. The rust-streaked mobile rested on a precarious foundation of fieldstones, through which numerous cats and hounddogs circulated in perpetual pursuit. Half a dozen vehicles sat around the mobile home in various stages of dismantling for parts. An old manuel washing machine with three legs leaned against a railing of the ramshackle porch.

Shannon recognized most of the people as Cogers or their relatives, although several local townspeople gawked at the family from outside the barbed wire enclosure. Most locals seemed to have their eyes fixed on two KHOG-TV newswagons and their crews.

"I--I don't really know why I'm crying for Connie," Shannon said shakily. "Most of her life seemed even sadder than her death. It just all seemed so unjust and undeserved..." She choked to a stop, unable to continue.

Her mother responded in a wobbly voice, "Just such a waste though. . . someone with her whole life ahead. I cry for the chances she never had."

"Life ain't fair," Jim Ceranda declared huskily. "That girl never had no chanct atall with that daddy of hers. When you're young, it's easy to let your problems get all out of proportion." He hugged Shannon again, obviously feeling her pain.

"That's mostly what I'm crying for--that I didn't help her get it in proportion. I should've reported that cult leader even if he did threaten us." She broke into sobs once more, and her father cradled her against his chest as she confessed her encounter with FOU to her astonished parent.

"Making mistakes is a big part of growing up," he soothed. "Whatever you did probably wouldn't have changed the outcome. Terrible forces were activated in Connie's life probably before you were even born that only she could harness."

They became silent along with the waiting crowd as a hearse approached in a cloud of dust. The portly driver dismounted, trying to hold his swallowtailed coat around his belly in the gusty wind as he went to open the gate to the cemetery. Brother Vanderhorn, the Pentecostal minister, came out from the tiny chapel to shake hands with the undertaker. Then the undertaker's helper, dressed in a black suit, climbed stiffly down and joined the minister and undertaker, walking with them to the plot where Connie was to be buried. The spectators watched in almost total silence, eyes wide and solemn. With the attention of everyone focused on the cemetery, a second hearse arrived almost unnoticed in a swirl of dust, parking behind the first.

Shannon's father held onto his Sunday hat, peering at the second hearse. "H-m-m, they must be going to bury Randy here too." he surmised. "I thought he might have a military funeral. But maybe with a dishonorable discharge, he didn't qualify."

A very tall man in a black suit and hat dismounted from the driver's side of the second hearse. His assistant hopped out and opened the back of the long coach. All at once, six bearded men sprang from the back of the older hearse and scurried to open the back of the first coach. Shannon and her parents exchanged alarmed glances as they reappeared carrying two bodies.

Jumping in his pickup, Jim Ceranda began honking frantically, motioning the undertaker toward the second hearse which had wheeled around and was racing away toward Kingsville. The fat little man raced for his hearse and left with such speed that one of the caskets slid out the back and disintegrated before the shocked spectators. For the first time, most of the crowd became aware of the unfolding drama.

"I heard they weren't having a regular funeral procession because they feared that cult might try to steal the bodies and fake a reseurrection," Jim Ceranda said looking around wildly. "There comes the police escort now! Jo, you tell them what happened, and I aim to follow that grave-robber."

"Oh, please don't, Jimmy." his wife pleaded, climbing out reluctantly as he raced the motor, motioning her out.

"You too, Shanny," he ordered. She closed the door behind Jo.

"I'm going with you," she insisted with that stubborn gleam of the eye he recognized as irresistible. Grabbing the rifle from the rack behind the pickup seat, she said grimly; "You know I can shoot better than you." Jim Ceranda peeled out hearing his wife yelling at him to be careful. Down the road, he saw the new hearse circling back. The driver motioned for Jim to pursue, which he was already doing as fast as his Silverado would run, Before the dust from the chase had completely settled on the crowd at the cemetery, police and highway patrolmen joined the chase, peeling off like killer bees from the area near the mobile home where they had congregated to plan crowd-control tactics. Both news vans followed.

As the television crew waited for traffic to clear for take-off, one of the cameramen videoed a toothless woman, talking behind her hand to another: "Woman, ain't no tellin' what'll happen to that pore youngun. I heered them cult fellers have sex with the dead."

"Shoot, I been doin' that with Henry for years." the other retorted. They stifled their smiles when they saw the camcorder.

CHAPTER XXVIII

The old hearse took the Devil's Den State Park Exit off Highway Seventy-One South on two wheels. Shannon and her father did the same, close enough now that she could see the bearded mountaineers kneeling beside two burial boxes through the dirty windows. Shannon looked back anxiously, hoping to see police or highway patrol cars behind them that would witness their exit. None were in sight. In a few minutes, they entered an area beyond the park that became like a dark tunnel through the forest's thickets, where the trees seemed woven thatch-like to shut out the sun. Briars covered the bushes at roadside, rendering them impassable. Jim Ceranda maintained his speed doggedly lest the body snatchers take a side road and escape.

Becoming more and more anxious as they bored deeper into the forest, Shannon checked the supply of shells in her rifle and in the pickup. After it seemed they had traveled at breakneck speed for miles, she kept glancing over her shoulder. Finally, she cautioned, trying not to betray her anxiety.

"There's no sign of the police, dad. Do you think we might oughta wait for them to catch up? There's seven or eight guys in that hearse and probably more guns than that. Are you sure you know what they're capable of doing to us?"

"I know," he said stubbornly, "but damned if I want the creeps to escape." He slowed down for a moment, adding, "Keep your eyes peeled. Surely the cops aren't far behind. . ."

"Unless they thought we headed on down Seventy-One," she said, heart lurching at the thought.

He took his eyes off the narrow trail for a second to see if she appeared terrified. "I'll stop if you're afraid," he offered.

Eyes blazing with excitement, she shouted, "Look at that!" Pyramids of rocks topped with Satanic symbols lined the road, Some bore metallic pentagrams; some had twisted crosses. With their attention focused on the weird altars, the pickup hurtled around a sharp curve, almost rear-ending the old hearse. To the left, Shannon saw a two-story, Hindu-style temple of stacked pyramid-shaped structures, whose shelves held statues of reclining men and women engaging in intercourse. Almost obscuring the temple, a pyramid towered beside the road. Until one of the mountain men jerked the pickup door open and dragged her struggling to the ground, she did not see that the top of the earth pyramid appeared to have been flattened to contain a grave and headstone. Another giant subdued her father, dragged him out.

Bearded men seemed to swarm from every direction. But not until Shannon recognized the tall man in black as MostHi FOU did she know the ultimate liquidity of terror over her whole body. Her bones seemed to soften like spaghetti in boiling water. Her body tried to crumple, but his branded right hand grabbed her, holding her upright.

He tossed his hat back into the hearse and moved like a greedy vulture carrying her with his cape blowing like wings behind him. The overhead rays highlighted the tatooed serpent on his bald head. He bowed, his eyes mocking her as he caressed her salaciously.

"Ah, so," he hissed, "we meet again, Lady of the Flaming Tresses!" He studied her, stroking his pointed goatee. "I knew my powers would draw you back to me. My blood pulses in your veins, willing you to be as sensual as MostHi Father of the

Universe. It is inevitable." She recoiled, cowering back against the side of her father's vehicle. MostHi FOU wet his lips, his slanted eyes glittering as if he enjoyed her fear.

Seeing two of the mountain men dragging her father away, she pleaded, "You won't let them hurt my father, will you? Oh, please." Her voice broke, turning into a wail. I must control myself or they will kill both of us, she thought, bracing her body to stop its quaking.

For the first time in her life, Shannon saw her father's face distorted with terror. The bearded men were strapping him to an altar behind the pyramid. Falling at MostHi FOU's sandaled feet, she begged once more for her father's safety. "I'll do whatever you say if you just won't hurt us," she said, trying to look meek until a better opportunity presented itself to escape.

Grabbing her, he pulled her roughly to her feet, holding her hard against his body until she felt his physical response on her pelvis. His expression reminded her of how he had thrust his finger into the pelvis of the skeleton. She shivered, involuntarily.

"You've thought of me a lot since we last met," he said, his eyes willing her to agree. Smelling the strong odor of alcohol, she understood why his slanted eyes appeared bloodshot, unnaturally dialated, and his speech slightly slurred.

MostHi FOU's dark eyes held hers as he produced leather thongs and bound her hands and feet. Towering over her, he seemed even more than his eight foot stature as he gloated: "I prefer to control my women through the mind. But with new converts, especially wilful redheads, I rely on physical restraints for awhile." Memory of his icy words after revealing the skeleton echoed down the dark corridors of her mind as she tried to imagine what fiendish scheme occupied his thoughts: "Women have always had to pay for their pleasure with pain."

Bending over her, he dropped a black velvet hood over her head. As her senses reeled, she realized it contained chloroform. Her last fading mental picture was FOU's cruel mouth repeating: "You will now sleep and dream of awaking to rapture with me such as you have never known, little virgin." *How did he know I'm without sexual experience? If he really reads minds, I'm d-e-a-d.*

CHAPTER XXIX

Shannon's first disorientation began to dissipate as she listened to the sounds around her. Feeling over her velveteen hood, she discovered a small breathing hole at the back which she cautiously twisted to afford a dim view of her surroundings. As she suspected from the musty smell and the damp rock floor on which her bound body lay, they had brought her back to the scene of her first meeting with MostHi FOU.

MostHi FOU stood spotlighted in the center of the cavern, wearing jewel-bedecked turban and robes. He looked like a Maharajah's picture Life had once carried as part of a series on international wedding customs. He even wore the gold-embroidered slippers with curled toes. Oh, God, please don't let me be the bride, she beseeched, quivering at the thought.

The wide-eyed mountain men resembled a tree-full of owls as MostHi FOU gestured toward something on the cave floor. Cautiously moving in order to see what so awed the bearded ones, she felt her scalp tighten. Connie's nude body lay spread-eagled on the limestone slab. Her alabaster white body had been placed on a crude wooden cross. Her slender arms extended in the form of a cross, nailed through both hands to a two by four. Her feet and legs were lashed to another timber that ran the length of her body and appeared to be fastened to the crosspiece. Overwhelmed, Shannon could scarcely comprehend, yet tried to concentrate on the words of her captor..

"Even the scriptures in the book called Revelations testify to the power of MostHi Father of the Universe," his resonant voice thundered. "And it shall come to pass just as this scripture predicts: After three and one-half days, the spirit of life will re-enter my witnesses. And great fear will fall upon our enemies. Today, you saw how helpless the police proved to be, and how fearful those who had ridiculed our beliefs became when we rescued those who will testify to my power by their reseurrection at the appointed time." The mountain men applauded and yelled.

Looking at Connie blew her mind totally. The girl could not weigh ninety pounds and scars or bruises covered her skeletal remains. Shannon averted her eyes and prayed as FOU's voice drilled into her eardrums,shutting her mind to the probability of what lay ahead.

"As your Bible predicts in Revelations, Seven-Eleven, after one thousand two hundred sixty days of witnessing, my followers will die but be raised to immortality.

"Again, Revelations, Chapter Thirteen testifies: 'And the Dragon gave him his own power and throne and great authority.' Yes, brethren, The Great Dragon gave MostHi power to fight against God's people, to avenge our banishment from his kingdom." His sawtooth smile changed to a sneer as he added, "The Most Beautiful Angel of all, The Lovely Lucifer, has appointed MostHi, part of the Trinity,to be the one to overcome these self-righteous hypocrites who pretend to hold the keys to the worldly kingdom, denying men the sensual things their bodies crave, good sex, good drugs and perfect health."

His voice rose and became more menacing as his maniacal gaze raked the circle of intent faces. "Before we are halted, all mankind shall become blood brothers and sisters with the Lovely Lucifer, the Great Dragon and Father of the Universe."

Walking over, he stood astride Connie's crucified corpse and lifted his arms in triumph. "All you who share my blood, bow now before the Father of Ubiquity!" His compelling eyes searched the crowd to be sure that every head had bowed.

Shannon's blood ran cold at FOU's calculating manipulation of these ignorant people. Now she knew for sure the truth of the saying: "The Devil can quote scripture to suit his own purposes."

Dropping his purple robe, he lowered his body over the girl's until nothing could be seen of her but the cross with which his thrusts beat a rhythm while his followers cheered. He rose, seeming to glory in their applause before he donned his robe. Then, he bowed mockingly toward the crucifixion:

"So much for my obeisance to the Cross!" declared the necrophile.

The room hushed as FOU turned and stared toward the shelf where Shannon lay frozen with horror. She felt those eyes burn like live coals through her clothing, but she pretended to still be unconscious.

"I see our latest convert is still in the arms of Morpheus," he drawled. "But I can tell you men that this one is indeed a virgin, unlike our last." The men laughed and he went on with a lecherous leer in Shannon's direction, holding up a long-nailed finger, "At least from the best I could determine with this." When he licked the finger, smacking his thin lips, Hank Baadshaw fell on the floor laughing. The cave magnified their raucous revelry as MostHi FOU told his followers to help themselves to the drinks and drugs.

After they had all become roaring drunk and Shannon was fighting hysteria, MostHi FOU rose and announced with a menacing glance to where she faked sleep: "If this young virgin refuses to honor her blood vow to become one with MostHi, we will conduct the ritual of the virgin. I have propitiated volcanoes and stormy seas with such all over the world since I, myself, was cast into a burning pit. My followers may choose the site of the next ritual or construct their own pit of fire."

Suddenly, Shannon felt something crawling on her hand. Glancing down, she saw a stinging scorpion poised to strike the place where her blue vein showed through the transparent skin. She shrieked instinctively, and all the red eyes focused on her.

CHAPTER XXX

A call from the Madison County Sheriff sent Bill Madden, the Newton County Sheriff, and his deputies careening toward MostHi FOU's hang-out from all over the mountainous terrain where they had been on patrol. They found the narrow hollow and the temple deserted except for Jim Ceranda, who lay bound and gagged in an old cellar. When Sheriff Madden tried to question Ceranda, he appeared incoherent from drugs or from the bloody gash that creased his gray mop of hair.

"You got any other leads about where that riff-raff can hide out?" one deputy asked the other two. They shook their heads.

"I'm fixin' to get on the radio and check the different roads to see if anybody has spotted that hearse," Sheriff Madden said, climbing into his Jeep. "In the meantime, you guys try to get some coffee down ole Jim and try to find out if he has any notion where that weirdo took his daughter."

Before Madden finished checking out leads, Dallas Villines' pickup pulled up beside the sheriff's vehicle. In the cab with Dallas were his wife and Shannon's mother. Although Josephine

Ceranda's eyes were red-rimmed in her tear-splotched face, she had gotten beyond crying. Sheriff Madden went around the pickup and placed a big hand awkwardly on her shoulder.

"We found Jim, and he's O.K., Jo!" he said. "Oh, he's been walloped with a gun butt, looks like, but he's going to be fine. We're trying to get some coffee down him to see if he knows where they took Shannon."

Mrs. Ceranda gasped and grabbed her heart. Monty's mother hugged Jo as she began to sob. "You've got to be strong for Jim," she suggested. "let's go see if we can help with him."

"He's going to die for sure when he learns they took our Shanny," Jo wailed, "I can't bear to even say the words."

One of the deputies called down to the sheriff as he reached the top of the pyramid! "Ain't nobody in this grave up here but Jesus." They all looked at him open-mouthed, and he added hastily, "I mean a statute of Jesus."

"If you'll see that Jim gets to a doctor, me and my men will start following up the one lead we got as to where they might be hiding," the sheriff offered, tilting his stetson down to shut out a ray of the setting sun that had leaked under the heavy foliage. "Gonna be down-dark 'fore we know it, and I shore would like to get that turkey in my coop 'fore he does any more dirty work."

"Sure, we'll take care of Jim," Dallas Villines assured him. "You just get that little girl back safe and sound."

CHAPTER XXXI

Monty Villines skillfully negotiated the curves of the mountain road into his parent's Flying "V" Ranch just as his mother returned from leaving the Cerandas at the hospital in Harrison. Delighted and surprised, she held her stalwart son close for a second, dreading to tell him about Shannon. When she did, alarm seemed to banish instantly his travel fatigue.

Dashing to his room, he returned with his dad's holstered guns, presented to him at graduation. Then he took a long flashlight from the tackle room and checked it to be sure the batteries were charged. His mother watched his busy preparations warily, hoping she might be wrong about his plans.

"You're not joining that posse too, I hope," she said. "I can't risk losing you and your dad too. You know he'll be right behind Sheriff Madden?"

He nodded grimly, but before she could protest more, added: "No, I'm not joining them, but I have something I have to do."

She knew from the square set of his jaw that protesting was useless as he ran for his pickup. His tires wailed a banshee farewell, and she sighed.

Darkness had fallen by the time Monty parked his vehicle by the old farmhouse near Skull Cave and climbed the mountain opposite the bluff with the cave at its base. Ghostly vapors hung tattered garments from weathered crags around the top of Skull Bluff. The full moon emphasized the cliff's eerie resemblance to a human skull. From near the top of the opposite mountain, the white limestone flying buttress above the maw of the cave resembled a nose bone, and openings on either side of the verticle limestone ridge—the eye sockets. Snaggle teeth of stalactites and stalagmites inside the cave mouth gave the appearance of a greedy monster waiting to devour him as it had more than once in his nightmares.

He stopped to regain his breath, sitting near house-size lichen-covered boulders. Checking his father's old Colts, he felt the familiar surge of cold fear as he strapped the holster around his waist. Reaching the well where they had exited the cave previously, he looked down the slimy sides of the deep cistern, jumping involuntarily at the moon's reflection in the water. He felt thankful he had thought to bring a rope from his pickup as he removed the coil from around his shoulders and knotted it securely around a sapling by the well curb. Fastening his father's lighted flashlight to his belt and grasping the rope, he felt for the first mossy rock step with his boot.

"Slick as snot," he muttered as his boot slipped off and his hold on the rope kept him from plunging down the shaft. Still clinging to the rope, he scraped hard with the steel-toed tip of his boot, hearing the moss hit the deep water below with a sickening "kerchug".

He hesitated, trying to recall even one of the three hundred sixty-five quotations from the Bible about fighting fear. His mental computer display read: "Fear not, for I am with you always, even to the end of the world." That oughta cover this situation, he thought, swallowing hard several times and breathing deeply to help reduce his nervousness.

Bringing this rope was an inspiration from above, he reassured himself. *If Shanny's hurt, I can lift her out with it.* The thought strengthened him as he started the descent. *But I mustn't allow myself to think of what that psycho may be doing to her or I'll lose my cool and plunge to my death. Or that I made the wrong decision about their whereabouts. Oh Lord, let me just concentrate on the next step and trust you to guide my feet a lot better than I have been.*

When he stepped through the door into the utter dank darkness of the cave, he reminded himself: No one but you knows about this rendezvous spot for the cult. *You may be the thread by which Shanny's life hangs. The boulder is over against the wall, so you must have guessed right. God help it to be so!* Keeping his flashlight beam pointed downward, he removed his boots and crept along the damp passageway, stopping to listen every few feet, hearing nothing but crickets and the beating of his own heart.

Once, he slipped and went sprawling, skidding several feet down a watery stretch of stone. He lay there for a long time, holding his breath until he began to black out from oxygen deprivation, He took long deep breaths trying to regain his lost composure, refusing to obey every basic instinct that told his body to run as fast as possible for the exit. Every sound became magnified by the acoustics in the tunnel until his breathing sounded like the beat of a bongo drum. He heard something that sounded like distant applause, but finally convinced himself it must be cicadias.

Finally, he regained enough strength to proceed on his quaking legs. But he hadn't gone far until he heard the unmistakable sound of voices. His chaotic senses sorted out the sound of MostHi FOU's menacing bellow followed by cheering. *It wasn't cicadias after all. Oh God, I hope I'm wrong about what those fiends are applauding.* Then he came far enough around the curving tunnel wall into the cavern to see a woman's nude body nailed to a cross, and he found himself going insane with a rage that shook him to his physical and mental foundations. He cocked the gun, remaining in the shadows. The attention of FOU's followers seemed so intently focused on something over by the shelf of rock, that he stood there with relative immunity from detection. They cheered once more, and he realized their rukus had likely covered the noise of his fall back in the passageway.

He stepped forward around the column of stone at the cavern entry, holding his cocked gun. Within six feet of him stood MostHi FOU, looking taller even than his eight feet in the tall turban with its glowing Cat's Eye Pin. The monster flung back his purple robe, reversing it to reveal the black lining, turning it into a cloak that hung down his back. Preening, he strode back and forth before his followers, stroking himself until the serpent of his loins created its own weaving shadow as part of the gigantic darkness created by MostHi FOU.

Monty felt as if he had turned to stone himself from the rage and revulsion that consumed him. He stayed rooted to the stone floor as FOU performed a salacious thrusting dance toward the shelf where he had displayed the skeleton..

Only when he heard Shannon's terrified cry, did he realize that the crucified woman was not Shannon.

"Aha!" MostHi FOU gloated, "I see the little virgin is begging for my attention!"

"Yow, Man, give 'er soma that mare serum like you done Connie!" yelled one of the mountain men.

This coarse yell triggered such fury that Monty lunged into the light, blazing away at FOU first. MostHi FOU grabbed his wounded arm and fled with his cloak streaming behind him like wings. When Monty turned the gun toward the mountain men, they were already scrambling from their perches and fighting for right of way through the narrow tunnel. He fired over their heads at MostHi FOU's white hindquarters that had become a dim white blur down the tunnel and saw him fall.

Dropping the smoking revolver, he hastened to loosen Shannon's bonds with his pocket knife. Lifting her to her feet, he held her close until she could stop quivering and sobbing. When he held her away, he gloried in the way those gorgeous green eyes devoured every detail of Monty Villines. Lifting her off her feet, he held her very close, breathing against her hair, "Thank God! Oh, Thank God!" I can't believe I'm really holding you! My heart almost stopped at first glimpse of poor Connie. In the darkness, I thought it was you!" She felt his tears beading on her upturned face and gently brushed his chin.

"It would have been me in a few minutes," she said, snuggling against his chest, loving the feeling of one-ness, of finding her destined sanctuary. "I still can't believe my' prayers were answered—even better than I dared to ask."

"You told me once there was a master plan for us," he said, looking down at her, his voice full of emotion, visible tears in his dark eyes.

"And this has to be part of it. Otherwise, how did you know to look here?" she asked wonderingly. "Even hear about the kidnapping?"

"I read about the suicide in Nashville and headed home, hoping to stop it. Had car trouble. You name it. It's a long story, but anyway, I got home just as Mom returned from taking your dad to the hospital and he's fine."

"W-h-e-e!" she rejoiced. "This whole thing just blows my feeble mind!" Sobering, she forced herself to look at Connie's body. Wincing, she hid her eyes against his denim jacket. "It was my dream to save her," she said tremulously.

"Mine too," he said, looking around the littered cavern. Removing his jean jacket, he tenderly covered Connie's body. "We've got to find Randy's body. I suspect it's around here. Then we gotta do what we shoulda done in the first place--get the Law after this scum."

"I can't believe it took all this to make my dream come true," she said huskily, seeking the shelter of his arms once more. "To see you and be in your arms once more."

"You aren't going to be much of any place else if I can help it," he vowed, kissing her eyes, her throat, her lips.

When she could breath normally again, she teased: "You don't have to worry about me being Jail Bait any more."

"I never did," he said, "Like I told you before, I only wanted to scare the other guys away from my girl until she became my woman." He laughed at her expression of mock dismay. "I have to say though I'll never be able to give you the unconditional love you wrote that you wanted."

With raised eyebrows, she asked, "What do you mean? Why not?" *May he always look at me with such possessiveness and pride,* her thoughts beseeched.

"Because, I can only love you with the condition that you'll be mine forever," he whispered, kissing her once more.

Holding hands, they raced for the exit.

THE   END

The author was born Dorothy Garton in the Ozark Mountain area that provides the setting for this novel. She enlisted in the Air Force in 1944 and ran a typing pool of young Indian men in Karachi, India, near the end of World War II. In 1992 Dorothy Cariker Cart was named Oklahoma's Woman Veteran of the Year to honor her overseas service, as well as to recognize her over six thousand hours of volunteer work at a Veteran's Hospital. She has written many novels, short stories, poems, a screen play and a teleplay.